DOMINANT SA

Club of Dominance 2

Becca Van

MENAGE EVERLASTING

Siren Publishing, Inc.
www.SirenPublishing.com

A SIREN PUBLISHING BOOK
IMPRINT: Ménage Everlasting

DOMINANT SAVIORS
Copyright © 2013 by Becca Van

ISBN: 978-1-62740-015-2

First Printing: April 2013

Cover design by Harris Channing
All art and logo copyright © 2013 by Siren Publishing, Inc.

Printed in the U.S.A.

PUBLISHER
Siren Publishing, Inc.
www.SirenPublishing.com

DOMINANT SAVIORS

Club of Dominance 2

BECCA VAN
Copyright © 2013

Chapter One

Tank eyed the small brunette as she stood quietly next to the tall, muscular man he presumed was her Dom. She was so tiny and petite, the top of her head didn't even reach the shoulders of the man beside her. Her head was lowered and her hands were clasped in front of her, but her body language told him she didn't want to be here at Club of Dominance, and maybe she didn't want to be with the man beside her.

He wondered what sort of relationship she had with the man at her side. Was she his girlfriend as well as his sub? He studied her surreptitiously as Aurora, the receptionist at Club of Dominance, went through the club rules with the "so-called" Dom. The guy with the petite woman stood a little less than six feet tall, with a lean, athletic physique, but his body language was all wrong. Tank didn't like the way he stood so aggressively, with his hips jutted forward and his jaw clamped tight and his chin pushed out. The asshole glared at Aurora as she explained the club rules.

Aurora obviously didn't like him either, because she moved in closer to Tank's side, unconsciously seeking protection and comfort. Tank placed a hand at her back and rubbed soothingly, letting her know he was aware of her discomfort. He shifted his gaze back to the little woman at the asshole's side. She was quite a beauty with her shoulder-length auburn hair and petite but curvy body. Her eyelashes were long and curved, nearly resting against the pale skin of her cheeks. She shifted slightly, and he noticed how she clutched her fingers together so hard that her knuckles were white. Definitely a couple to keep an eye on. Something just wasn't right about the pair. He wondered if maybe they were only in a weekend Dom/sub relationship. He hoped so.

The woman called on all his male instincts of protection as well as his dominant tendencies. But what surprised him the most was that his cock was sitting up and taking notice. His penis had begun twitching behind the fly of his black jeans as soon as he had sighted the small woman.

She had on a red leather miniskirt and a black corset which pushed her breasts up so high they were in danger of spilling out of the top. She looked like she was having trouble breathing and he glanced down to see that her corset had been pulled in too tight. The poor thing couldn't even take a deep breath, just short little pants, but her eyes never rose from the floor and she didn't look like she was about to complain. And since he'd had no interest in a female besides playing occasionally with an unattached sub in the club, he decided he wanted to get to know this sub much better. He just hoped that the little one wasn't attached to the asshole at her side.

"I know all the rules regarding Doms and their subs. You don't need to tell me any more."

Tank slid his eyes over to the asshole when Aurora took a step back. He had planted his hands on the counter and was leaning over antagonistically and glaring at Aurora.

Tank gently grasped Aurora's hips and moved her back a couple of steps. Then he stood in front of her so the asshole couldn't see her. He felt her little hands clutch the back of his T-shirt for a moment, and then she rubbed his back as if trying to soothe him.

"Every Dom and sub is to be told the rules of Club of Dominance." Tank drew on his full six-foot-four height as he glared at the asshole. Trying to intimidate the prick, he crossed his arms over his chest, knowing that his large biceps bulged even more. "Master Turner Pike makes sure that everyone understands the house rules. It is imperative that each person who enters through these doors understands that the policies are, and always will be, safe, sane, and consensual and that we allow no sadomasochism.

"You and your sub are to read the club policies and then sign at the bottom. That way there can be no litigation since everyone who enters the club understands the rules. Every Dom and sub in this club is to be treated with the utmost respect." Tank narrowed his eyes and was satisfied when the arrogant ass moved back from the counter. Tank handed him the papers and then turned to the woman, but he kept the prick in his peripheral vision, studying the elfin sub while the bastard filled in the papers.

Her face was pale, and perspiration had formed on her upper lip and forehead. She gripped her fingers so tightly now that they were starting to turn as white as her knuckles. Tank watched as she tried to draw a deep breath into her lungs, but he could see she was in trouble. She began swaying on her feet as if she was about to pass out.

"Aurora, get Master Turner and Master Barry out here now." Tank didn't bother trying to skirt around the end of the counter. There wasn't time. Right at this moment he had never been so glad for his military training and the fact that he kept up his physique with martial arts and weightlifting. He placed a hand on the counter and jumped over it with ease. Just as his feet landed, the auburn-haired woman's legs buckled. Tank grasped her around the waist and lifted her slight weight into his arms. She whimpered as if she was in pain, which made him shift his hold on her. The last thing he wanted to do was hurt her.

"You stupid bitch." The asshole turned toward Tank and reached out to grab the woman's arm in a cruelly bruising grip. "I told you to drink that water before we arrived here. Can't you do anything right?"

Tank wanted to knock the fucker's hand off the woman but until he knew what was wrong with her, he didn't want to jostle her around too much by holding her with only one arm.

"Let her go. *Now!*" Tank roared and knocked into the jerk with his big body. It was enough to make him release the woman's arm and send him staggering back a few steps. He looked down to see red marks he knew would leave bruises on her creamy white skin. Just as he was about to give the prick a piece of his mind, the interior doors to the club burst open.

Turner and Barry came rushing into the lobby.

"What's going on?" Turner asked.

"I'm not sure yet, but this one isn't well. This asshole doesn't even seem to care that his woman is sick."

Turner took in the sight of the woman in his arms, and his mouth tightened in anger when he saw the red finger marks on her upper arm. He walked toward the fucker and glared at him before snatching the papers from the asshole's hand and gave them a glance.

"Mr. Andrew Mitchell, you aren't given permission to enter this club. In fact, you will never get in here. Please leave."

Mitchell's fists clenched and his jaw tightened, but when he took a step toward Tank and the woman, Turner and Barry moved forward and blocked him. Barry crossed his arms over his chest and Tank wished he could have seen his friend's face. Whatever he did scared the shit out of Mitchell, who backed toward the door, never taking his eyes from Barry.

"Make sure he leaves without causing any problems, Barry," Turner said, and Barry followed the fucker out the door.

"Do you want me to take her?" Turner asked as he walked over to him.

"No, but we need to get her into a bed and out of her clothes. Her corset is so tight she can barely draw a breath."

"Follow me." Turner headed toward the inside entrance to the club but stopped before he opened the doors. "Are you okay, honey?"

Tank glanced back at Aurora and saw she was sitting in the chair behind the counter, her hand on her chest. Aurora nodded but didn't speak. "I'll send out Master Mike to sit with you for a while."

Aurora's face flushed and she looked away then she glanced at Turner and nodded.

Tank followed Turner through the club, skirting the Doms and subs and around the small dance floor in the middle. The sounds of the club, women screaming in ecstasy, the slash of floggers, and the pop of palms hitting skin faded into the background as he stared at the unconscious woman in his arms.

He'd felt her body go lax when the front doors had slammed behind that asshole. Her face was covered with perspiration and she looked flushed. His worry increased as shivers wracked her body. He could feel the heat emanating off of her as he held her against his chest.

"She's sick," he said. "Is Jack here?"

His best friend and one of the two men he shared a house with was a GP, but Tank hadn't seen him since this morning. Jack sometimes got to the club early enough to relax after a harrowing day in the ER.

Turner glanced over his shoulder. "I'll find out. If he's at the hospital, we can call someone else."

Tank nodded, though he would rather not. He'd served with Jack in the military, and they'd been practically inseparable ever since. Tank would rather entrust this woman to him than to a stranger.

He followed Turner to the back internal door which led to Turner's private rooms, waited impatiently while Turner keyed in the code, and then followed him to the guest suite off the hall. Tank walked to the bed and gently placed his small bundle on the mattress. When he rolled her onto her side so he could get at her corset laces, he drew in a ragged breath and growled with fury. The skin above her top was red with raised welts that, in his haste, he had not yet noticed.

A few of them still seeped blood. No wonder she was sick. The poor woman had to be in agony.

"Fuck," Turner snarled as he, too, saw the woman's marred, cut skin. "Call Jack. He was in one of the seating areas talking to some of the other Doms."

"Thank God." Tank removed his cell from his pocket and hit speed dial. He used his free hand to begin working on the knot which held the woman's corset closed.

"Hello?"

Tank was relieved to recognize the music in the background as the same song that had been playing on the dance floor. "You're at the club?" he asked without prelude.

"Yeah, I'm in one of the sitting areas. What's—"

"Get your bag from your car and come to Turner's guest room. We have a very sick sub on our hands." Tank didn't wait for Jack's reply. He disconnected the call and tried to undo the knot in the string, but it was too tight for his large fingers.

"Have you got a knife handy?"

Turner went to the small kitchen area and came back with a knife in his hand. "You cut her corset away while I hold her steady. We don't want her getting cut if she wakes up."

Tank carefully slashed through the strings on the corset and drew the sides apart. He drew in a gasp when he saw the marks and blood on the woman's back, and a growl rumbled up from his chest and out through clenched teeth. A beep sounded and Tank realized it was Jack at the door asking permission to enter Turner's private area.

Turner rushed from the room and was back in seconds with Jack at his side.

"Fuck!" Jack snarled when he saw the woman's back. "Who did this to her?"

"We'll talk later, just help her. She has a fever and she passed out." Tank carefully shifted her onto her stomach, making sure her head was turned to the side so she could breathe easily.

Turner called his sub on his cell phone. "Charlie, I need you to get the digital camera and bring it into the guest suite…Thanks, baby."

Jack nudged Tank aside as he opened his bag and got to work. He cleaned her wounds carefully, and when Charlie entered the room, Tank took the camera and snapped picture after picture, making sure he photographed all the damage done to the little sub. Charlie started crying when she saw the battered woman, and Turner pulled her into his arms to offer her comfort. With his help, Jack had bandaged her up with gauze before long. After they had her injuries covered, Jack prepared two shots.

"Jesus," Barry said as he entered the room and stood next to Turner, pulling his upset sub from Turner's arms into his own and hugging her while rubbing a hand up and down her back. "I wish I hadn't let that fucker go."

"We all do," Turner replied.

"I'm injecting her with an antibiotic as well as a painkiller. Hopefully she won't wake up again tonight. I think she probably just passed out because she couldn't get enough oxygen, but she also seems to be exhausted. It's no wonder considering what she's been through. Get Gary in here. I want him to see this, and when she wakes up, he can take her statement. Whoever did this should be arrested for assault."

Turner pulled out his cell and made the call to Gary Wade. The other man Tank shared a house with was a detective. He could help them document the woman's injuries to hopefully put that asshole Mitchell behind bars. When Turner nodded at him and Jack, Tank knew it wouldn't be long before Gary showed up.

"Tank, help me get the rest of her clothes off and get her into bed. We need to make her as comfortable as possible." Jack gently lifted her hips, and Tank placed an arm under her upper body below her breasts. He levered her up and pulled the remains of her corset out from beneath her. After gently lowering her back down, he saw the edge of what looked like a card protruding from a hidden pocket on the inside of her corset. He pulled it out, and with it came a wad of cash which had been wrapped around her license.

Tank studied the photo and then looked at her name. Emma Macintosh, age twenty-four and a resident of Tigard. He passed Emma's license over to Turner, who then handed it to Barry. When the bell sounded, Charlie left the room to let Gary in. Gary took in the room's occupants with a glance and walked over to the bed.

"What's the problem?" Gary asked as he stared at the unconscious woman.

Turner handed over the camera without a word. Gary's demeanor changed from relaxed to taut within moments as he scrolled through the pictures. "Son of a fucking bitch. Who did this to her?"

Turner reached into his pocket, pulled out some papers, and handed them over. They must have been the club rules that Mitchell partially filled out. Barry handed her license over, too. "We suspect the Dom she was with hurt her, but we can't prove anything."

"Fuck." Gary spun away and began pacing and then turned back again. "I know this asshole. He's been up on assault charges before. He pretends he's a Dom and lures in innocent women and then he works them over. I'll get someone to pick the fucker up." Gary moved out into the hallway as he pulled his cell from his pocket and flipped it open, but Tank knew until Gary got Emma's statement, if she was willing to give one, the asshole couldn't be arrested, just brought in for questioning.

"I made note of his license plate." Barry walked out into the hall to recite the number to Gary before returning to hold Charlie tight.

Tank glanced back toward the bed when Emma moved and gave a moan of pain. He sat on the edge of the bed opposite Jack and stroked her hair, trying to convey comfort and safety. Her eyelids fluttered open, and she blinked a few times as if her vision was blurry. She had the sweetest, most soulful brown eyes he had ever seen, but it killed him inside to see them glazed over with fever, pain, and medication. No doubt the drugs Jack had given her were beginning to work.

"Shh, Emma, you're safe now, darlin'. He can't hurt you anymore."

Emma whimpered and blinked again, and then her muscles tightened and her breathing escalated. Before he could stop her, she sprang to her hands and knees and crawled up to the top of the bed. Tears leaked from her eyes and tracked down over her white face. She moaned with pain but didn't stop moving until her back was up against the wooden headboard. She flinched and drew her knees up to her chest, wrapping her arms around her legs. Her eyes darted around the room as she took in all the men.

"Emma." Tank spoke firmly, hoping the sound of his voice would get through her fear. When her eyes landed on him, he kept talking. "You are safe here, honey. No one is going to hurt you. Mitchell has gone and won't get near you again." He held a hand out to her and waited to see if she would take his offer of help. "Why don't we get you back under the covers, darlin'?"

"Emma," Jack said quietly, "I've treated your wounds and given you some antibiotics and painkillers. I'm Jack Williams, a GP. This is Anton Taylor, but everyone calls him Tank because he's such a big bastard. I promise no one will harm you, sweetie. Come and lie down until those painkillers kick in."

Tank wanted to pick her up and hold her in his arms, but he knew that if he made any sudden moves, she would try to scramble farther away, and he didn't want her to put more pressure on her back. Some of the welts must be turning infected if Jack was prescribing an antibiotic and Emma had a fever. God knew how long she had been in the clutches of that fucker. He wondered if the asshole had kidnapped her and, if she was missing, if someone had reported her disappearance to the police. As much as he wanted to know, this wasn't the time to hammer her with questions.

Her eyes were glazed over and she seemed to be having trouble focusing, but when Gary entered the room again, she used her feet to push into the mattress, pressing her back against the headboard. Gary must have seen her fear. He halted in his tracks.

Charlie withdrew from Barry's arms and moved closer to the bed. She smiled at Emma and nudged Jack away, making room to sit closer to the frightened woman.

"Hi, Emma, I'm Charlene but everyone calls me Charlie. Would you like to lie down again? You don't look so good." Charlie slowly reached out and rubbed Emma's foot. When she didn't flinch away, Charlie kept right on offering the woman comfort.

"I promise that you're safe here. No one will hurt you. We want to help you."

Seeming totally oblivious to the fact that she was nearly naked, Emma slowly released one of her arms from around her legs and grasped Charlie's hand tightly. "I have to leave. He will come back and kill me. He told me if I didn't please him tonight then he would slash my throat."

Tank felt the fury rising up inside him but didn't let it show since he didn't want to frighten Emma any more than she already was. He glanced over to the other men and saw the same rage in their eyes, but they, too, kept their expressions blank.

"He can't get to you here, Emma. You're safe, I promise." Charlie kept her voice soft, but Tank could see the pain she tried to hide at Emma's condition and her terror.

Gary stepped toward the bed but halted again when Emma sobbed and cringed away. Her eyelids were so heavy she was barely keeping them open. Tank knew it wouldn't be long before she finally succumbed to the effects of the drugs. Her head sagged slightly and she blinked. Her lids struggled to open again, and she only managed to open them to mere slits. Then her head slumped backward, and she began to sag.

Tank caught her before her head could connect with the wooden headboard, but she was unconscious before he even touched her.

He looked up at Jack and Gary. His friends' faces were pale. Tank knew exactly how they felt as he looked back to the woman in his arms.

What did he do to you, little one?

Chapter Two

Jack was so full of rage he didn't know how he had kept it hidden from little Emma Macintosh. He wanted to hunt down the asshole who had hurt her and kill him with his bare hands, and that was so against his own caring personality it worried even him. When Emma finally gave up the fight against the painkillers he'd given her, he sighed with relief and then turned toward Gary.

"I want to know everything there is to know about her. Where her family is, who she works for, and how long that fucker had her."

"I'm already on it, Jack. God, I can't wait to get hold of that fucker." Gary glanced toward the sleeping Emma. "She is so damn petite it's a wonder he didn't kill her."

"As far as I can tell, the damage was done with a whip, at least recently," Jack said. "There are no signs of broken bones, but she had a few bruises on her legs, too. God knows what she's had to endure."

"We have to keep her safe," Tank said with a sigh. "I think she really believes that Mitchell will kill her if he gets his hands on her again."

"I do, too," Gary said. "He's escalated from his last assault. Once she's awake, I'll get a statement. Did she say anything to any of you before she spoke to Charlie?"

"No," Jack answered and turned to Tank.

"No. She didn't speak at all. If she hadn't begun to sweat and then pass out she would still be with that motherfucker."

"No, she wouldn't." Turner stepped forward and drew Charlie back into his arms when she moved away from the bed. "You know that every monitor in this place would have stepped in as soon as that asshole had removed her corset."

"He's right," Barry said. "That bastard wouldn't have lasted five minutes in here."

"I'm just fucking glad that prick brought her here. At least I was able to treat her and we all know she's safe, even if she doesn't." Jack rose to his feet and began to pace. He looked over at his two best friends and housemates, Tank and Gary. They looked just as livid as he felt, but he saw the underlying yearning when they, too, looked at Emma. It seemed they were drawn to the petite woman, too.

He pushed those thoughts aside. What mattered most at the moment was getting Emma well and keeping her safe.

"I want to stay with her," Tank said as he sat on the side of the bed and stroked the hair back from her face.

"Me, too." Emma was such a pretty little thing. Even under the room's harsh fluorescent lights, the light red strands in her shoulder-length, chestnut-colored hair glinted. He wanted to lean over and kiss the creamy white skin of her delicate shoulders and work his way up her slender neck and over to her lush lips. Even though she was small in stature, Emma was all woman, with curves and dips in all the right places. He had glimpsed her lush breasts after he'd treated her injuries. He would almost believe they were too large for her petite frame, too heavy for such a small woman to have to carry. They would fill his large hands perfectly. Her breasts were full and perky, and to him she was absolutely perfect.

Jack mentally cursed and pushed his lust aside. The last thing little Emma needed, was his and Tank's arousal being obvious to her and making her run.

Movement close by caused him to turn and meet Gary's eyes as his friend came closer to the bed.

"She's beautiful, isn't she? Shit, what makes a woman stay with such a bastard?" Gary scrubbed his hand over his face as if weary. And Jack figured he probably was. He dealt with this sort of shit on a regular basis. He was a hard-assed Dom but he was also one of the most protective people he knew. Gary was the first to jump in without a thought to his own safety in protecting the innocents of the world.

"Who said she wanted to be with him?" Tank rose to his feet, moved across the room and snagged an armchair, then pulled it close to the bed and sat down. "You yourself said that you know this Mitchell fucker. Who knows how they met, but I don't think she seems the type to stay with someone who would abuse her."

"He's right, you know," Turner said as the others began to clear the room. Charlie left with Barry, and Turner was moving toward the door, too. "Don't jump to any conclusions about little Miss Emma. Wait until she's awake and then question her. I believe I can leave her in your capable hands?"

"You know you can." Jack waved him away. "We'll take good care of her."

Turner studied him and then Tank and Gary. "Yes. I believe you will. Call me if you need anything." Turner left.

"So what are we going to do?" Tank looked at his two friends.

"We take one step at a time," Gary said, not taking his eyes off of Emma as he sat on a chair across the room.

Jack sat back in his chair and settled in for a long night. Emma was going to need a lot of caring to help her heal.

*   *   *   *

Emma whimpered as the asshole strapped her cuffed wrists to the chain hanging from the ceiling in the center of the room. His green eyes were blank of all expression and chillingly cold, and even his smile was full of malevolence. Her panic and fear increased. She was so scared she could barely get enough air into her lungs as her breath panted in and out of her open mouth, rushing past her teeth. Shivers and shudders wracked her body, and her trembling legs felt so weak she wondered how she was still standing on her toes.

He turned away and walked over to the wooden bench on the far side of the warehouse and rummaged around for something. When he spun back around she could see the evil and insanity in his eyes. He lifted his hand and bared his teeth at her. Emma's eyes dropped to his hand. She tugged against the restraints as fear permeated her body and her heart beat so hard and fast she wondered if it would burst out of her chest.

The leather cuffs at her wrists burned her flesh as she pulled and twisted, trying to get away from him, but she couldn't get any purchase as he had her on the very tips of her toes. Even though she knew her efforts were futile, she couldn't give up. She had to escape or she would die trying. A hysterical bubble of laughter formed in her chest and traveled up her throat to escape her mouth, sounding like a wounded, laughing hyena. The light from the bare bulb above her head shone on the metal in his hand, and tears ran down her cheeks.

He stopped in front of her. She looked into those evil, blank eyes and saw her own death. She screamed when he raised the scissors toward her and then screamed again as he began cutting her clothes away from her body. His laughter was a grating, malicious sound which scraped her already ragged nerves.

Her clothes fell away, leaving her feeling cold, vulnerable, and exposed. Her skin crawled as he ran his eyes over her body. She felt so dirty. She shuddered with fear, and her legs buckled as the scissors in his hand moved toward her once more. He chuckled as he cut away a lock of her hair and then brought it to his nose, sniffing. Pain radiated from her shoulders and down her arms, the only things holding her suspended weight up. When he walked away, she sighed at the temporary reprieve and was able to get her fear under control. He was back at the bench, and she prayed to God that someone would find her and help her.

Please God. Please save me.

Emma sobbed as he strode back toward her, resolve and aggression in every step. He had what looked like a whip in his hand.

Oh God. Please. *He stopped in front of her and stared into her eyes and then he winked at her. Nausea roiled in her stomach. He moved again, walking behind her, and bile rose in her throat with terror and anxiety.*

What's he doing? Oh please God. Help me!

The whoosh was almost drowned out by the pounding of her own heart and panting breaths, but the crack was loud even to her ears. Emma screamed in pain as the lash landed and fiery hot agony radiated out across her back. She screamed over and over as the thick leather landed again and again. Her back was a mass of burning hurt, and she felt small trickles over her agonized flesh. She was bleeding. It felt like he had cut her back wide open with each lick of the whip against her sensitive flesh. Her body was hot, and yet she shivered with cold. Please, please, please.

He released the cuffs from the chain, and she slumped against him. She didn't want him holding her, but she couldn't stand on her own. Her shoulders ached, and her hands began to tingle as blood flowed back into her limbs. She tried to push him away, but she was so weak and in so much pain that she had no strength left. He picked her up and carried her to the bed in the corner of the room, dumping her there. She screamed as her tortured back connected with fabric.

She couldn't see. She wondered if she had closed her eyes. The blackness of her vision spread into her mind, and she gratefully sank into oblivion.

* * * *

When the first whimper left Emma's mouth and she struggled in her sleep with the quilt covering her, Gary jumped up from his chair and rushed over to her side. Her scream pierced the air and she sat up, her arms flailing as tears ran down her face. Her eyelids were open, but he knew she wasn't seeing the here and now from the glazed look in her eyes.

"Jesus," Gary said as he grabbed her arms above her bruised wrists so she wouldn't hurt herself. Tank had beaten him to the bed and had her over his lap, trying to restrain her, too. He moved around to stand in front of her in case Tank needed help

She kicked out and pegged him in the chest with her little feet, screaming again and again. Jack was on his feet at the side of the bed, rummaging around in his bag, and he came up with a needle.

"Hold her still!" Jack barked out the order but Gary was already on it. Tank had wrapped his arms around hers as well as her chest so she couldn't move her upper body. Gary gripped her ankles and held them down until he could crawl on the bed. He straddled her legs and carefully used his weight to keep them still. She didn't stop screaming and struggling, but between him and Tank, they had her restrained. Jack swabbed her upper arm near her shoulder and then pricked her skin and plunged the medicine into her body. After a few minutes, her struggles lessened and she finally slumped in Tank's hold.

Gary shifted off her legs and sat on the side of the bed. "What the fuck did that asshole do to her?"

Tank shifted out from behind her and lifted her up into his arms. Between the three of them, they got her settled on her side and covered her up with the quilt. He sighed with relief at her deep, even breathing, a testament to the sedative working at calming her panicked nightmare.

"Have they picked that fucker up yet?" Jack asked as he carefully disposed of the needle in the small sharps bucket he always carried in his bag.

"I would have heard if they had."

"You think he's run?" Tank asked as he settled back in the chair at the bedside.

"That would be my guess," Gary said with a sigh. "Until we have her statement I can't put out an APB on him. We don't have any proof of what he's done. At the moment he's only a person of interest. Shit. We're gonna have to wait until she wakes up, and then there is no guarantee that she will want him to be arrested. Did you check her for sexual assault?"

"There weren't any signs to say she had been raped," Jack snarled and then ran his fingers through his hair. "Sorry. I wanted to check her over more thoroughly, but until she is conscious I didn't feel right about doing that."

Gary nodded. "Yeah, I can understand that. She probably already feels like she's been violated. Until she wakes there's not much we can do. How long will that sedative work?"

"Normally just a couple of hours, but we'll have to wait and see. Who knows how her body is going to respond to what it's been through. I'd say he's had her for a couple of days from her injuries but I could be wrong." Jack shrugged.

"I doubt it," Gary replied. "You're hardly ever wrong when it comes to anything medical."

"Maybe," Jack sighed.

Tank settled back in the armchair and stared at Emma, concern for the little woman emanating from his face. Jack sat as well and closed his eyes. Within moments his breathing had evened out as he dozed. Being a doctor and having served in the armed forces, he'd learned to nap just about anywhere, just as Gary and Tank had. But Gary was still too angry and pent up to sleep. It was going to be a long night.

Chapter Three

Emma was so warm and comfortable she didn't want to move. Her back was still sore, but the pain had lessened. *Thank you, God.* She was in that place where sleep and wakefulness came together, but she didn't want to open her eyes and face her nightmare again. *Where is he?* She listened intently as her body pulled her to consciousness, but she couldn't hear anything. Hopefully he had left her alone and she could try and escape.

Shit. She hated that she had been one of those people who was paralyzed with fear and couldn't think straight. She had always thought that she would fight until she breathed her last breath. But no, it turned out that she was an utter coward in the face of adversity. Tears leaked from the corners of her eyes and she sniffed.

A rustle off to her side caused her to freeze once more. Her heart rate escalated, as did her breathing, but something was different. The tight band which had been around her breasts and torso was gone, and she was actually able to fill her lungs with air. Her muscles tensed, and she bit her lip to keep a whimper from escaping when she heard another sound close to her other side.

Oh God, is there someone else in here with him? Please.

Emma, you have to find some courage and get out of here. Who even knows that you're missing? God, I don't even know what day it is. Everything is such a haze.

She bit her lip so hard she tasted blood. Taking a few deep breaths, she tried to get her fear under control, and some of the tension left her muscles. A hand touched her forehead and Emma snapped. She opened her mouth and screamed loud and long as she hit out and scrambled from the bed. Almost blind with terror, she leapt from the bed and ran. Almost at once, she slammed into a hard, immovable object. Large, muscular arms banded around her chest, but she kept right on fighting and screaming. She dug her nails into the arm and kicked out with her legs. A grunt sounded as her feet connected with another hard body. *Oh fuck, there are two of them.* Nausea roiled in her stomach and bile traveled up her esophagus. She barely stopped herself from vomiting.

And then a loud voice penetrated her mindless panic.

"Emma! You're safe, sugar. Calm down, honey." Large, gentle hands cupped her cheeks. "Shh, Emma, you are safe here. He can't get to you again. We won't let him near you. I promise."

She slowed her struggles. The red haze of fear finally began to clear from her eyes, and she blinked moisture away. Her vision cleared. Standing before her was a stranger. But he was looking at her with such worry and concern it tugged at her heart. His thumbs moved across her face, and he wiped the tears from her cheeks.

"That's it, sugar. Take deep, even breaths. You are safe, Emma."

Emma looked into the darkest eyes she had ever seen. They were such a deep brown color they were almost black. His hair was also a deep brown, and messy as if he had run his fingers through his hair all night long. Whoever he was, he was big. Not only was he bulky with muscle, but he stood a few inches over six feet. Although she should have been afraid of his size, she wasn't.

The arms around her loosened and shifted to her waist as she steadied on her feet. She looked over her shoulder and met green eyes way above her head. The man standing behind her was even bigger than the one in front of her, at least six five. His sandy-colored hair was collar length, and he was linebacker huge with muscles. The heat from his body was oddly comforting and his large hands were gentle on her waist and hips.

Seeing movement in her peripheral vision, she turned her head and stared at the blond-headed, blue-eyed man across the room. He wasn't as tall as the other two or as muscular, but he was still ripped from what she could see. He smiled at her as if trying to put her at ease, but she could still see worry in his eyes.

Who are these men? Where am I?

She shifted on her feet and the man behind her released her waist. His hands slid over her naked skin. Looking down, she gasped when she realized she was almost naked. The only item of clothing she had on were her panties. She stepped off to the side and away from them, crossing her arms over her chest to hide her breasts from view.

The guy who had been in front of her and had drawn her from her panic backed up a couple of steps, and then turned and pulled the quilt from the bed. He stepped toward her and stopped when she drew away.

"Take it easy, sugar. We aren't going to hurt you. We want to help you. Here." He held the end of the quilt up in offering.

Emma took a tentative step forward and slowly reached out for the blanket. Gripping it tightly, she pulled it around her, covering her body with its softness. "Who…"

"Why don't you sit down, Emma, and then we can talk," the man with the dark eyes said.

She shook her head and backed away until her shoulders connected with the wall. Pain shot through her, but she contained the shudder that traveled down her spine.

"Who are you?"

"I'm Detective Gary Wade and these are my friends. The big guy is Anton Taylor, but everyone calls him Tank. The blond over there is Dr. Jack Williams." Gary moved back and sat on the edge of the bed. Jack lowered himself into a chair on the other side of the room and Anton leaned against the wall with his arms crossed over his massive chest. His muscles bulged with each slight movement he made.

"Where am I?" Emma croaked.

Jack stood again and walked over to what looked like a kitchen area in the room. He poured a glass of water and then turned back.

"I'm coming over to give you this drink, Emma. I promise not to touch you or get too close. Okay?"

Emma eyed the water and nodded. She looked up into Jack's blue eyes and held her breath as he crossed the room. Tentatively taking the glass from his hand, she waited until he had retreated before bringing the glass to her lips. The first taste was pure ambrosia, and she couldn't stop herself from gulping the contents from the glass.

"Do you want some more water, baby?"

Emma whipped her head around and stared at Anton, but relaxed when she saw that he hadn't moved from his lounging position against the wall. She nodded her head and watched him warily as he straightened and walked toward her.

She frowned because she could have sworn she had heard his voice before. She looked up into his green eyes and frowned again, because even though his voice was somehow familiar, Emma knew she would remember him if she had met him previously.

"Do I know you?"

"We met last night, baby. Don't you remember?" Anton took the glass from her hand and handed it over to Jack.

"Your voice sounds familiar, but I don't remember you."

"You came into the club with that Mitchell guy, but you were sick with a fever so I guess you were pretty out of it."

"Club? What club?"

"Why don't you come and sit down, Emma?" Gary asked, indicating the large armchair near the bed. "You need rest to heal properly."

If she hadn't felt so tired, she would have refused, but she made her way toward the chair carefully so she wouldn't trip on the quilt and then sighed as she sat down.

"Good girl." Gary studied her face but he didn't move from his perch on the bed. "Can you tell me what happened to you, Emma? I need to take a statement so that when we find Mitchell we can arrest him."

Emma opened her mouth but snapped it closed when the door to the room burst open. She jumped as it slammed into the wall behind. Two more men followed another woman into the room.

"Oh, you're awake. Thank God. We've all been so worried about you." The woman rushed over and patted the hand that was peeking out the top of the quilt where Emma was clutching it closed. "How are you feeling, Emma?"

"Okay."

"You don't remember me, do you?" the woman asked with a smile. "I'm Charlie Winston-Pike and these two big lugs are my husbands. This is Turner Pike and Barry Winston."

Did she just say husbands? No, I must have heard wrong.

"Hi, Emma. I'm glad you're feeling better."

"Hi, Emma. Thank God you're safe."

Emma didn't know what to say. She didn't even know these people, so she kept silent.

"Why don't we leave these four to talk," Turner said to Charlie and clasped her hand in his own and began to lead her from the room. "We'll get breakfast ready and call you all when it's done." Turner, Charlie, and Barry left the room, closing the door behind them.

"Emma, you are in the Club of Discipline. That asshole you were with last night brought you here. Do you remember what happened?"

Emma stared at the three men watching her. They were all so big and handsome and could hurt her easily, but she knew they wouldn't. They said she was safe with them and she believed them. The big guy, Anton, no, Tank, had helped her get away from *him*. If these men had wanted to hurt her, they wouldn't have helped her in the first place. Gary pulled a small pad and pen out of his pocket, and she knew he was waiting for her to give him a statement.

Why had she agreed to go on a date with him? He'd seemed so nice, had spent the last four weeks talking to her at work. She should have known something wasn't right. A couple of times she had caught him staring at her, but she had just put that down to his attraction toward her. How wrong she had been. She pushed her thoughts aside and tried to concentrate on what she had to say.

"Andrew and I work together in an insurance company call center. He sat a few cubicles away from me, but we began talking when it turned out we had the same breaks." Emma shuddered and took a deep breath.

"It's okay, sugar. You are safe here," Gary reassured her.

"He was so nice to me, and after we had shared the same shifts for four weeks running, he asked me out to dinner. And foolish me, I said yes."

Tank had been standing at the end of the bed holding the glass of water, which he seemed to have forgotten about as he listened to her. When he looked down, he frowned and then walked over to hand her the glass.

"Thanks." Emma stared into the glass, but she was aware of the three men nearby. Jack had moved his chair closer so he could hear, and now Tank sat on the bed next to Gary.

She took a sip and then continued. "He was to pick me up Friday night at seven and then we were going to a restaurant. But we never did get to eat. He took me to an abandoned warehouse which had been set up with a bed." A shiver wracked her body as she remembered the chains hanging from the ceiling, and she took a deep, steadying breath. "As soon as I saw the chains dangling from the ceiling, I began to get nervous. He was standing behind me, and as I decided I wasn't staying and turned toward the door, he grabbed my hands and pulled them over my head. I should have screamed and fought, but he just stared at me so coldly and I was so scared I froze." A sob escaped, but she took another deep breath and told the three men how he handcuffed her and chained her arms up and then how he'd stripped and whipped her.

The memories assailed her once more, and even though she continued to talk, she was once again lost in terror.

* * * *

Emma whimpered as the asshole strapped her cuffed wrists to the chain hanging from the ceiling in the center of the room. His green eyes were blank of all expression and chillingly cold, and even his smile was full of malevolence. Her panic and fear increased. She was so scared she could barely get enough air into her lungs as her breath panted in and out of her open mouth, rushing past her teeth. Shivers and shudders wracked her body, and her trembling legs felt so weak she wondered how she was still standing on her toes.

He turned away and walked over to the wooden bench on the far side of the warehouse and rummaged around for something. When he spun back around she could see the evil and insanity in his eyes. He lifted his hand and bared his teeth at her. Emma's eyes dropped to his hand. She tugged against the restraints as fear permeated her body and her heart beat so hard and fast she wondered if it would burst out of her chest.

The leather cuffs at her wrists burned her flesh as she pulled and twisted, trying to get away from him, but she couldn't get any purchase as he had her on the very tips of her toes. Even though she knew her efforts were futile, she couldn't give up. She had to escape or she would die trying. A hysterical bubble of laughter formed in her chest and traveled up her throat to escape her mouth, sounding like a wounded, laughing hyena. The light from the bare bulb above her head shone on the metal in his hand, and tears ran down her cheeks.

He stopped in front of her. She looked into those evil, blank eyes and saw her own death. She screamed when he raised the scissors toward her and then screamed again as he began cutting her clothes away from her body. His laughter was a grating, malicious sound which scraped her already ragged nerves.

Her clothes fell away, leaving her feeling cold, vulnerable, and exposed. Her skin crawled as he ran his eyes over her body. She felt so dirty. She shuddered with fear, and her legs buckled as the scissors *in his hand moved toward her once more. He chuckled as he cut away a lock of her hair and then brought it to his nose, sniffing. Pain radiated from her shoulders and down her arms, the only things holding her suspended weight up. When he walked away, she sighed at the temporary reprieve and was able to get her fear under control. He was back at the bench, and she prayed to God that someone would find her and help her.*

Please God. Please save me.

Emma sobbed as he strode back toward her, resolve and aggression in every stride. He had what looked like a whip in his hand. Oh God. Please. He stopped in front of her and stared into her eyes and then he winked at her. Nausea roiled in her stomach. He moved again, walking behind her, and bile rose in her throat with terror and anxiety.

What's he doing? Oh please God. Help me!

The whoosh was almost drowned out by the pounding of her own heart and panting breaths, but the crack was loud even to her ears. Emma screamed in pain as the lash landed and fiery hot agony radiated out across her back. She screamed over and over as the thick leather landed again and again. Her back was a mass of burning hurt, and she felt small trickles over her agonized flesh. She was bleeding. It felt like he had cut her back wide open with each lick of the whip against her sensitive flesh. Her body was hot, and yet she shivered with cold. Please, please, please.

He released the cuffs from the chain, and she slumped against him. She didn't want him holding her, but she couldn't stand on her own. Her shoulders ached, and her hands began to tingle as blood flowed back into her limbs. She tried to push him away, but she was weak and in so much pain that she had no strength left. He picked her up and carried her to the bed in the corner of the room, dumping her there. She screamed as her tortured back connected with fabric.

She couldn't see. She wondered if she had closed her eyes. The blackness of her vision spread into her mind, and she gratefully sank into oblivion.

Emma whimpered as hands pulled and tugged at her. He slid panties up her legs and then fastened a short leather skirt around her hips. She cried out when she was rolled over and then screamed as something was pulled tight around her breasts, torso, and back. God, how long is he going to torture me? How long before he kills me? How long have I been here? I don't know how much more I can take. Please, let me die.

"Get up," he snarled and pulled her across the bed by her arms. Emma swayed on her feet, her vision blurry with pain and dizziness. He shoved her feet into shoes and then grasped her arm and pulled her out the door. She wanted to fight, but she was too weak and scared to say or do anything. She was frozen inside with fear and in too much pain to see. He shoved her into a car and buckled her in. Her limbs were feeble, and she was in so much discomfort she felt sick. A shiver wracked her body and she managed to move her arms to hug herself.

How long had it been since she'd eaten or had a drink? She licked her lips, but it didn't help much. The car stopped and she realized she had her eyes closed. God, Emma, find some strength and courage. You have to get out of this or you're going to die.

He shoved a bottle into her hands, and she managed to open her eyes wide enough to see what it was. Water. She wanted to open the cap and guzzle the whole bottle down in one go, but she wasn't about to make it easier on him. In a fit of pique she dropped it. He cursed and then laughed evilly as he dragged her from the car. The pain in her back was so intense that nothing she saw registered in her brain.

"If you give me any trouble I will beat you, rape you, and then slit your throat," Andrew whispered through clenched teeth, pulling her along with a bruising grip on her arm. She automatically walked up steps and then stood still when he told her to. Noise registered in her

brain but she couldn't work out what she was hearing. She gripped her fingers so tightly her knuckles ached. His voice grated on her nerves, and she shuddered. Was he talking to someone?

Sweat formed on her upper lip and she stared unseeingly at the floor. Whatever was around her breasts, ribs, and back was so tight she could hardly get a breath. She heard a thud and then a muscular arm was around her waist as her legs buckled. Emma didn't hit the floor like she expected, and darkness once again formed on the edges of her mind. A hard hand gripped her arm with bruising force, and then she heard someone yelling. A door slammed and then she knew no more.

* * * *

By the time she'd finished, she was crying again.

Strong hands pulled her from her chair, and she found herself snuggled up in a firm, warm embrace and on someone's lap. She felt safe for the first time in what seemed like forever, and all her fear and emotions came out in wrenching sobs. Her crying finally calmed, and she became aware of a hand rubbing up and down her arm through the thick quilt and of the calm voices talking to her.

"Shh, sugar. He can't hurt you again."

Emma finally sat up and looked into Gary's dark eyes. "What day is it?"

"It's Monday morning, Emma."

"Shit. I missed work. I was supposed to have the early shift."

"I'll take care of that for you, Emma. Tell me where you work and I'll get a couple of my officers to go and see your boss. We need as much information on Andrew Mitchell as possible. It's not the first time he's assaulted a woman, and he wasn't at home when they went to pick him up. His car was still in the driveway, too."

"You think he's on the run?" Emma asked Gary.

"Yeah, I think Tank, Barry, and Turner scared the shit out of him, but until we know for sure, I don't think it's safe for you to be alone. Do you have any family you can stay with for a while?"

Emma shook her head. "There's just me."

"What happened to your family, sugar?" Gary asked gently.

"Um, they all died in a plane crash when I was seventeen. We were all supposed to go on vacation, but I got sick. I told my family to go, and I stayed with my friend Sally since she was sick, too. The plane crashed, killing my parents and sister."

"I'm sorry, Emma. That must have been hard on you. Did you have any other family to take you in?"

"No. I stayed with Sally and her family for a couple of months. They were good to me and I finished school, but I didn't feel right staying there too long. Sally's family had money problems and four kids of their own to take care of, so as soon as I was able to, I got a job and moved out on my own. I learned to take care of myself."

"Such a brave little girl," Jack said from behind her.

"Not really." She looked at him over her shoulder. "I just did what was necessary to survive."

The door to the room opened, and Charlie entered with a bundle in her hands. "Breakfast is ready, guys. Why don't you go and make a start while I help Emma get dressed?"

"Okay." Gary kissed Emma on the temple. The action gave her a warm, fuzzy feeling, and when he lifted her and placed her to sit on the bed she felt...almost cold. The three men left the room. Jack looked back and winked at her just before he closed the door.

"Oh, you have those three Doms wrapped around your little finger already." Charlie tugged the quilt from Emma and then took her hand to help her to her feet.

"What?"

"Oh. Didn't you know that you are in a BDSM club?"

"Excuse me?" Emma asked, not sure she had heard right.

"Haven't you ever heard of BDSM before?" Charlie asked as she stopped in the bathroom and placed the bundle down on the vanity.

"Of course I've heard of BDSM, but I've never...I mean, I'm not..."

Charlie laughed and patted Emma on the shoulder. "Don't worry about it. That bastard brought you here and tried to sign you both up for membership, but when you collapsed, Turner and Barry kicked the fucker out."

He tried to sign up for membership? Emma had been too terrified back at the warehouse to think of what Andrew had done as anything other than torture. *Is that what BDSM is like?*

Emma eyed Charlie curiously. She wanted to ask if this cheerful, spunky woman could possibly be involved in BDSM. If she was at this club, she must be, but that made no sense to Emma. What sane woman would sign herself up for what Andrew had done? Emma considered herself lucky to even have survived.

Tears formed in Emma's eyes at that idea, and she blinked them back as she looked at the pretty Charlie. "I'll never be able to thank you all enough. I think he would have killed me eventually. I was so scared I was blind to my surroundings and frozen with fear."

"Hey, don't go getting all sappy on me or you'll have me in tears, too." Charlie gave her a careful hug. "Now why don't you clean up and get dressed. Jack said not to shower yet because of the cuts on your back. But you can wash up and brush your teeth and hair. At least then you'll feel semihuman, and after you've got some food in your stomach you should nearly be back to your old self again."

"Gee, thanks. I think," Emma said sarcastically.

"Oh, sorry I didn't mean..."

Emma laughed at the frown on Charlie's face, which changed to a smile. "I just know we are going to be good friends, Emma. I'll leave you to clean up. I'll wait outside, but make it quick because I'm hungry."

"Thanks, Charlie."

"You're welcome." The door closed with a quiet *snick*. By the time Emma had washed, dressed, and brushed her teeth, her stomach was growling loud enough to rival a hungry lion.

Emma hesitated in the door of the kitchen. She had followed Charlie out the door and down a long hallway and into a large apartment. But seeing so many big men all together made her nervous. Charlie must have realized she'd stopped because she turned back and came up beside her, took her hand, and whispered in her ear.

"No one here will hurt you, Emma. All the men in this club look out for women and would protect them with their lives. You are safe here. I promise." Charlie tugged her forward and led her over to an empty chair which was situated between Gary and Tank.

She sighed and leaned back, forgetting about her cuts and bruises. Emma yelped with pain and leaned forward again.

"After you've eaten I want to take another look at your back, honey." Jack smiled at her from across the table.

Emma nodded and stared at the food but didn't move to begin filling her plate. Her stomach let out another loud, unladylike growl, but she was worried if she began eating she wouldn't be able to stop. She was that hungry.

She caught Tank looking at her from the corner of her eye, and he picked up her plate and loaded it with pancakes, bacon, eggs, and toast. Emma was salivating by the time he put the full plate down in front of her.

"Dig in, Emma. We know you must be starving," Charlie said as she got started on her own food.

Emma cut into the syrup-covered pancake and shoved a piece into her mouth. She groaned as the sweetness exploded on her taste buds, and before she had swallowed, she shoved another bite into her mouth. She was so hungry she could have inhaled what was on her plate. Even though she didn't talk or look away from her food as she consumed it, she made sure she kept her manners on a tight rein. By the time she put the last bit of toast into her mouth, she was so full she didn't think she would be able to move.

She looked at Charlie to see the other woman grinning at her, and Emma gave a sheepish smile in return. "Thank you. That was delicious."

"You're welcome. Do you want a cup of coffee?"

"Please."

"Stay there, Charlie, and finish your breakfast. I'll get Emma's coffee." Jack stood up and walked to the kitchen. He was back moments later with a mug of coffee.

"Thank you, Jack." Emma smiled up at him. He surprised her by leaning down and kissing her cheek, and then he took his seat again. Emma reached for the milk and poured a little into her mug. When she lifted her head, she found three sets of eyes watching her intently. Gary, Tank, and Jack each smiled at her, and she glanced over to Charlie to find her grinning from ear to ear as she looked at Emma.

"What?" Emma asked, feeling a little uncomfortable at all the attention.

"Nothing," Charlie replied and then turned to talk to Barry.

By the time everyone had finished breakfast, Emma was feeling weary. She had a full belly after being so hungry, and all she wanted to do was curl up on a bed and go to sleep.

"Emma, why don't we go back to the other room so I can look at your back again?"

Charlie rose to her feet and began clearing the table.

"Oh, but I want to help Charlie first."

"No," Charlie said as she walked around the table. "Go and let Jack tend you. Master Barry and Master Turner will help me clean up."

"Did you just call them 'Master'?" Emma blurted.

She felt her face heat as all eyes turned to her. Charlie caught her expression and smiled, but Turner put a big hand on her shoulder and spoke instead. "Charlie is not only our wife but our sub, Emma. She calls us 'Master.'" He glanced at Charlie with a frown. "If she's being a good sub," he added.

Charlie's smile widened.

Emma blinked and opened her mouth only to close it again quickly, not wanting to look like an idiot in front of the others. Turner's explanation had raised as many questions as it had answered. Why did he keep saying "our"? Was she in a relationship with two men?

"Come on, Emma. Let's go." Jack took her hand in his and helped her to her feet. With a last glance at Charlie—and yes, it seemed she was in a relationship with two Doms, since Barry was kissing her on the mouth and Turner was hugging her from behind and nibbling on her neck—she let Jack lead her back to the room she'd spent the night in.

While they'd eaten, someone had come in and made the bed and tidied up. At the sound of the door closing, she spun around to see that Gary and Tank had followed her and Jack.

"Why don't you take your top off and lie on the bed on your stomach, sweetie?"

Emma was hesitant about being half naked with two other men in the room but knew by their crossed arms and dominant stances they weren't about to let her make them leave. She turned her back to them and pulled the top over her head, wincing when the action pulled on her tight, damaged flesh, but she made sure to keep her breasts covered by holding the shirt in front of her as she climbed on the bed.

"Now get comfortable, honey. I need to get those dressings off and apply more ointment, and then I'll give you another shot of antibiotics."

Emma held still while Jack removed the dressings on the cuts she'd sustained from her whipping and then again sighed with relief when the cream he applied to her injuries didn't sting.

"The cuts have scabbed over nicely and you should be able to take a shower or bath this evening. I'll get some waterproof bandages. In the meantime I think you should consider what you're going to do now." Jack taped more gauze to her back and then rubbed her shoulder. Then he prepared the injection, swabbed her arm, and slowly plunged the medicine into her arm. "All done, sweetie. Do you want help to get your shirt on?"

"No. Thank you, Jack."

"You're welcome, Emma."

Emma managed to get her shirt over her head and her arms in the sleeves while keeping her breasts pressed against the bed. Then, with a quick move, she rose up on her knees and balanced on one arm as she tugged the shirt down. When she turned around, she found three sets of male eyes watching her avidly.

Gary and Tank moved closer to the bed where the armchairs still were and sat down. Jack was still sitting on the side of the bed, and Emma scooted up until her back touched the headboard. After Jack's tender care the pain in her back had settled down some more, and she didn't flinch this time when it made contact with the hard wood. Her eyes connected with Jack's blue gaze.

"What do you mean about thinking over what I'm going to do now?" She glanced over to Gary when he shifted in his seat and then frowned at Jack. "I'm going to go home and get back to a normal routine."

"No, you're not." Gary spoke firmly.

Emma scowled at him and opened her mouth to argue, but Tank spoke before she could voice her opinion.

"Darlin', it's too dangerous for you to go back home and to return to work. Mitchell hasn't been caught and he could come after you again. You aren't safe until he's behind bars."

Emma knew he was right, but she didn't have anywhere else to go. Even though she had a lot of acquaintances, she didn't really have any friends, and she'd already told these men how her family had died. She felt lost, like she was adrift at sea without any way to control the direction she was headed. As she was trying to figure out what to do, a cell phone rang.

Gary answered the call and listened intently, all the time pinning her with his eyes.

Is that call about me? Why is he looking at me like that?

Emma couldn't believe the heat she saw in his eyes as he stared at her. She blinked a few times and mentally cursed when her body began to respond to that look. Crossing her arms over her chest as her nipples peaked, she tried to hide her reaction, which she prayed he hadn't seen. Lowering her eyes, Emma shifted on the bed and crossed her legs when her clit and pussy began to throb. Moisture leaked out onto her panties. When Tank moved, she glanced up to see that he was looking at her the same way Gary was.

Emma didn't like the way her body reacted to them and shifted over to the far side of the bed and rose to her feet. She took only a step before she bumped into a hard, warm male body. She glanced up into Jack's gaze and shivered when she saw he was also looking at her as if she was his last meal.

He gripped her upper arms and held her still when she would have backed away. It wasn't that she was scared of the three men in the room. What made her so nervous was the way her body was reacting to them, even after what she had just been through. What they saw in her she had no idea. As far as she was concerned she had always been small and plain—almost mousy in appearance, as she had been told by one of her male acquaintances.

"Emma, it's all right, sweetie. We would never hurt you."

"I–I d–didn't think you would," she managed to reply, albeit nervously, and licked her dry lips.

Gary snapped his phone closed, stood, and moved toward her. "You're coming home with us, Emma."

Chapter Four

Tank waited for Gary to explain his order, but his friend just stood near Emma with his arms across his chest and his feet planted shoulder width apart. His questions about the phone call Gary had just received would have to wait until later. From the tension in Gary's muscles, whatever he had learned couldn't be good, but he didn't want to question his friend in front of little Emma and upset her even more.

The little sub had no idea how expressive her face was, and the look of bewilderment as well as the sadness and apprehension which crossed her face almost tore his heart out. He wanted to pick her up and snuggle with her, but he didn't think she was ready for that just yet.

Tank was secretly glad that Gary had decided she was staying with them where they could make sure she was safe and keep an eye on her. Their property was twenty minutes east of Tigard, a large parcel of land with state-of-the-art security and a high fence around the whole estate, except where their land met the banks of Lake Oswego. Even the dock that protruded onto the lake had sensors which sounded an alert to all three of their cell phones if anyone set foot on the wood decking. No one could get in or out of the place without them being aware of it.

Jack released his hold on Emma's arms and stepped back when she gave him a shove, and then the little sub glared at Gary.

"What do you mean I'm coming with you? With which one of you?"

"Just what I said, little girl. You're coming home with all three of us."

"But…"

"No. There will be no arguing. You won't be safer than when you are in our home. We have state-of-the-art security. Mitchell won't be able to get to you there."

"I'm…"

"No, Emma, and that's final."

Tank hid his grin when Emma's eyes blazed with anger. She took the four steps needed to bring her closer to Gary. She shoved her finger into his chest and kept poking at his Dom friend as she let loose.

"You arrogant asshole. Who do you think you are, telling me what I can and can't do? You have no right to tell me what to do." By the time Emma had finished her short tirade she must have poked Gary at least ten times with her delicate little finger, and she was panting.

Tank was happy to see that Mitchell hadn't broken her spirit. He hadn't expected to get to see the real Emma Macintosh so soon, but he was glad she still had some fire in her.

Gary grabbed her finger before she could stab him with it again and then bent down until his face was level with hers. He leaned forward to touch his forehead to Emma's. "You're playing with fire, little one."

Emma gave Gary another scowl and then pulled her finger out of his grasp. She paced a few steps away and then spun back. "I can't stay with you. I have to work."

"That's all been taken care of, honey." Gary straightened to his full height and crossed his arms over his chest once more.

"What do you mean by that?" Emma snapped.

"I had some of my officers visit your workplace to question your boss about Mitchell. While they were there they arranged for you to have a leave of absence until that fucker is behind bars."

Emma stomped back over to Gary, placed her hands on her hips, and tilted her head back to frown at Tank's Dom friend. Tank counted in his head and waited for the fireworks, because he knew without a doubt they would be firing off at any second.

"How dare you arrange my life as if you have the right. I have to work to pay my bills, and if I don't work I can't pay my rent. I'm going home and there is nothing you can do about it."

"I wouldn't be so sure about that," Gary said.

Emma leaned back. She looked stunned more than angry, but she squared her shoulders and asked boldly, "If you make me go with you, how are you any different than Andrew Mitchell?"

Gary's jaw tightened. Tank sensed that his friend didn't like being compared to a man on the wrong side of the law. Tank stepped closer, and when Emma glanced at him, he said, "Because we care about your well-being, Emma. Mitchell wanted to hurt you." He held her gaze. "There are a lot of things we want, but that's not one of them."

Emma blinked rapidly. Tank could practically see the gears turning. But she didn't seem to be able to come up with a reply. Instead, she looked back at Gary, who was now wearing a smug grin. That apparently brought Emma's anger crashing down again. "God, you are so fricking arrogant," she said. "You make me want to scream." Emma slapped her palm on Gary's chest, moved around him, and headed for the door. Her hand was on the knob when she stopped, turned back, and looked about the room. When her eyes landed on her corset she stormed over to it and picked it up, obviously looking for her license and the cash she had stuffed in the secret pocket. How the hell she had managed to do that when she was being held captive and almost catatonic with fear whilst in Mitchell's clutches, Tank had no idea, but he intended to find out.

Before she could return to the door, Gary gripped her shoulders and turned her around to face him. "You aren't going anywhere but home with us, Emma. Your boss quite understood about you needing time off work. Especially when we told him one of his employees was the reason you need some time away. You don't have to worry about your apartment. I've arranged for your company to pay your rent while you are away. I've also got some police officers watching your place in case Mitchell shows up. One of the officers got the spare key from your landlord, and your clothing and personal items will be delivered to our house later this afternoon."

Emma stood staring at Gary with her mouth gaping open and fire in her eyes. She opened and closed it a few times before audibly snapping it shut. She looked so damn cute Tank wanted to go over there and kiss the fire and breath right out of her.

"How did you manage to get your license and cash into the bodice of your corset, when you were with Andrew Mitchell?" Tank finally asked.

"Don't change the subject," Emma said.

"Answer the question," Gary commanded.

His dangerous tone of voice seemed to startle her into honesty. "I didn't." Emma licked her lips. "He did. I don't know why he put money in the pocket, but I remember him saying that he needed to have my identification in case he was asked for proof of identity. If I had been more cognizant I would have tried to escape when we got to the club, but it was like my mind was filled with fog. I was in so much pain I could barely manage to draw breath, let alone be aware of my surroundings."

Gary pulled Emma into his arms, being careful not to put any pressure on her back, and held her against his chest. Tank saw her shudder, and Gary moved his hands down her sides and placed them on her ass, which was one of the only places on her back side besides her legs and arms that wasn't marred by the whip. "It's over now, baby. He won't get his hands on you again."

Emma visibly relaxed and leaned against Gary, seeming to draw some of his strength, and finally moved back a step.

Emma stood up straight and gazed into each of their faces in turn. When she met Tank's eyes, he saw how conflicted she was, and it was all he could do not to hug her, the way Gary had.

Instead he stood his ground and watched her. All of them had learned to read body language when they were in the military. Every little twitch and nuance was a tell to him and his friends. The skill served them well at the club, especially with someone like Emma, who wasn't good at hiding her reactions. He found her very easy to read. From her body's reaction earlier, he knew she was just as attracted to them as they were to her. She'd responded to their lusty stares, and right now she responded beautifully to their dominance.

"I'll go," Emma said. She lowered her gaze. "You saved me. And I don't actually think you're...like him." Seeming to remember how mad she'd been, she straightened again and gave Gary what she no doubt thought was a mean look. "But you should have asked me first."

As soon as Emma heals, Tank thought, all bets are off. Emma was the perfect submissive for all three of them and he couldn't wait to tap into the passion she had buried deep down inside her.

Jack walked over to Emma and took her hand in his. He looked down into her brown eyes, giving her a gentle smile. "Let's go, sweetie. The sooner we have you settled, the sooner you can rest."

Tank moved up to her other side and took her free hand in his. Her skin was cool and her hand so small that his large palm and fingers engulfed her flesh. She was a delicate little thing, therefore he and his friends were going to have to be very careful with her, once they finally got her into their beds. The last thing he wanted to do was cause her any hurt.

Gary took the lead out of the room and headed for the internal club door. Tank, Gary, and Jack had chatted with Turner and Barry while Charlie had been helping Emma get dressed. Turner and Barry had both agreed with them that Emma would be safer staying in their secure house and would be leaving after breakfast was over. Then they had each arranged for some time off from their various jobs. Tank had no trouble since he was part owner of the club with Barry and Turner. It had taken some fast-talking for Jack to arrange for vacation time, and although Gary had finagled some leave, he was still going to be spending some hours at the precinct as he and his colleagues gathered more information on Mitchell and tried to hunt the fucker down.

Now all they had to do was convince Emma they were the men for her. After what she had just been through with that sadistic bastard, Mitchell, that was easier said than done.

* * * *

Emma couldn't understand why she wasn't kicking up a fuss as she let Jack and Tank lead her down the hall. For some reason she felt safe and cared for, and she wondered if she'd had a mental breakdown after being kidnapped and whipped by Andrew Mitchell. But she pushed that thought aside because she knew she was lying to herself. She was physically attracted to the three big men but vowed they would never know it, although she wasn't sure if she had been as adept as she'd tried to be at hiding her arousal earlier.

Emma felt her eyes widen when they led her out the door and across a massive room. There were sitting areas screened off around the space, and a bald delivery guy in a brown uniform was unloading cases of bottled water behind the bar. Tank gave him a wave as they passed. But what snagged her attention the most was the weird-looking equipment she could see through the glass wall to her right, as well as the areas where the strange furniture and benches were out in the open. She glanced over the dance floor in the middle, and on the far side was a stage which had chains secured from hooks in the ceiling. They dangled down near the middle of the dais. She shuddered with fear because she knew how it felt to be chained up with no escape. When her eyes snagged on an X-shaped device and what looked like a padded saw bench, her shiver of fear turned to one of arousal. She could just imagine bending over that low bench with her ass in the air and masculine hands caressing her flesh.

Good God, girl. Are you crazy? You don't want these three men spanking you.

Do I?

She tried to push her crazy thought aside but then she remembered the many books she had read.

Since Emma indulged in reading erotic romance and a few of those books had been about BDSM, she knew what some of the equipment was for even if she didn't know the correct terminology for it. The only thing she knew the name for was a St. Andrew's Cross, the X-shaped apparatus which stood in a room behind the glass wall. Other than that, the furniture just looked like benches. *Maybe that's what they are—spanking benches.* A shiver worked its way up her spine, causing her to shudder and making goose bumps rise up on her skin. Her nipples pebbled into hard little points as if begging to be touched, and her breasts swelled and ached. She could just imagine being tied down to one of those things and having a hand connect with her ass. *What would it feel like to give up complete control, to have a man—or men—dominate my body with the goal of giving me pleasure?*

The hands holding hers seemed to tighten slightly, and she surreptitiously looked up to Tank and Jack from beneath lowered eyelashes to find them watching her. They both had grins on their faces, and Emma wondered if they had been watching the whole time they walked beside her.

Shit, you are going to have to learn to keep your thoughts and feelings better hidden, girl. She scolded herself for even feeling attracted to the idea. She would never allow herself to be in a helpless situation again.

Like you're not helpless now. Oh sure, she'd agreed to go with them, but she'd seen the look on Gary's face when she refused. Dominant men like these would have their way with her.

She shivered. Why did that turn her on so much?

Emma pushed those thoughts away as they neared the two large wooden doors. Gary opened and led the way out into the foyer of the club. Moments later she was outside standing in the parking lot and looking at three large trucks. Gary unlocked the black truck and opened the driver's door. "I'll take the lead. Jack, you take Emma with you and Tank can bring up the rear."

"Are you expecting trouble?" Tank asked.

"No. I don't think he'll make a move when there are three of us. Just make sure you keep a lookout for a tail. See you at home."

Jack guided Emma over to the navy truck and opened the passenger door for her, and Tank moved off to the red truck. She was about to try and climb up into the massive vehicle, but she didn't get the chance. Jack's hands gripped her waist and lifted her effortlessly, and then he climbed up onto the running board and buckled her in. His arm accidentally brushed against her breast, sending pleasure zinging down to her clit from her nipple. She didn't move until the door closed, and he walked around and got into the driver's side.

"Are you okay, sweetie?" Jack asked as he followed Gary's truck out the drive and onto the road.

"Yes."

"You're very quiet. Are you tired, Emma?"

Emma stifled a yawn and then realized that she was utterly exhausted. Why, she didn't know, since she'd only been awake for a few hours.

"Yeah."

"When we ask you a question, sweetie, we expect you to answer honestly."

Emma turned from the window and looked at Jack. He glanced at her but then concentrated on driving.

"I did."

"Yes, you did, but when I asked if you were okay, you didn't tell me you were tired. When a Dom asks a sub a question, he expects a full answer, not a half one. So instead of replying yes, you should have said 'yes, but I'm really tired.'"

Emma found herself speechless, and not for the first time today. Jack took in her expression with a glance, but he seemed to misunderstand the reason for her shock. "Are you familiar with the idea of Domination and submission?"

"Yes. I mean, no. I mean—I've read about it, but I'm not interested in it." For good measure, she added, "I'm not a sub."

"Oh you definitely are, Emma."

"How can you tell?"

Jack spoke as if he were considering his words carefully. "Our experience with Domination isn't from books. One thing I'll tell you for sure. No true Dom would harm his submissive. Tank, Gary, and I believe that women are to be loved and cherished. When we share a sub, she screams in pleasure, not pain."

Share. He said they share. She wondered if that was why they all lived in the same house. It had to be. Emma's head was spinning. It was all too much to take in.

"If you wanted to find that out for yourself," Jack continued, "you could."

"What?"

"You can let go around us, honey. We would never hurt you."

"I don't know what the hell you're talking about," Emma snapped and looked out the side window again.

* * * *

Jack didn't push Emma any more. He had planted the seed in her mind and he would leave it at that. What she needed the most now was rest and some TLC, and he and his friends were just the men to give it to her.

He knew they were going to have to be careful with Emma and not push her too hard or fast, but she already seemed comforted by their touch. That would help her heal.

Once she did, she'd be back to her normal, healthy, feisty self, and he couldn't wait for the sparks to fly.

Twenty minutes after leaving the club, he parked his truck in the garage and, after waiting for Tank to park next to him, he got out of the truck. Jack didn't bother to walk around to help Emma down because he knew Tank would beat him to it, since he was already at Emma's door.

Gary had already opened the internal door to the house and switched the alarm to home. Jack joined him and whispered for Gary's ears alone. "I've planted the sub seed."

"How did she take it?" Gary asked in a low voice.

"About as we'd expect."

Gary nodded that he understood and then headed toward the kitchen with Jack on his heels. Tank led Emma inside and then followed behind. Gary was already dealing with putting coffee on. Jack got mugs down but kept glancing over to Emma as she looked about. Once the coffee was made and they were all seated, Gary began to talk.

"That call I got back at the club was from one of my colleagues. It seems Mitchell is off the radar. He's probably hired a car and is using an alias. He must have had cash stashed somewhere because there have been no alerts set off on his credit cards."

"Damn," Tank muttered and then turned to Emma. "What do you know about Mitchell, honey?"

"Um, not much. He didn't talk about any family, just about some of his buddies."

"Did he mention any names, baby? Do you remember where the warehouse is or what type of car he was driving?" Gary took a sip of coffee.

"I don't know," Emma sighed and gripped her mug with both hands as if trying to absorb the warmth. "I can't seem to think straight at the moment."

"Don't worry if you can't remember right now, sweetie. Your mind just isn't able to cope with the terror you experienced. You need to rest, Emma." Jack reached over and cupped her cheek. "Finish your coffee and then I'll show you to your room."

Emma nodded and although she tried to hide by lowering her eyes, Jack had seen the moisture in them. He glanced at Gary and saw the concern in his eyes, too.

Jack knew it was going to take time before she got over what she had experienced with Mitchell. He realized she was probably going to be more emotional than she usually was for a while. There were dark smudges beneath her eyes, and he could tell by the tight lines around her face that her back was hurting her again. He just prayed that she didn't end up with nightmares as a result.

Time would no doubt tell them how deeply she had been affected by her kidnapping and torture.

Chapter Five

Emma lowered her head and leaned back in the chair. When her back connected with the piece of furniture she pulled her lips tight, trying to hold in her gasp of pain. Bad enough that she felt useless after not being able to answer Gary's questions. She didn't need to mess up the bandages Jack had put on her back.

She couldn't understand why she was feeling so emotional, but for some reason the kindness these three big, muscular Doms had shown her was getting to her. Emma had been independent for such a long time, and now that other human beings were offering her comfort and compassion after such a traumatic experience, she was barely holding it together.

Will I ever be able to laugh again? Will I be able to put this behind me?

Jack's voice drew her from her pity party. "I'll show you to your room, sweetie."

She took a deep breath as she tried to regain control of her emotions and blinked rapidly to dispel the moisture which had gathered in her eyes before she looked up.

Emma took Jack's hand and clung to it as if he was the only lifeline in a tumultuous storm. He must have felt her tension because he released her hand and wrapped an arm around her shoulders as he guided her from the room. He didn't say anything as he led her upstairs and down the hallway to the room at the end. If she hadn't been hanging on by a thread, she would have looked around the room and taken in her surroundings. But all Emma wanted to do was curl up on the bed and bawl her eyes out.

"Emma, look at me," Jack demanded in a firm voice which made her flinch. In all the time the three men had spent in her presence she hadn't heard that tone of voice from him before, and she wondered if she had somehow pissed him off.

"Now, Emma."

Emma raised her eyes and couldn't contain the tears any longer. They streamed down her face but she stood frozen, too scared to move, knowing if she did that she wouldn't be able to stop from shattering into a million pieces. And then she was in his arms. Jack bent down and swept her from her feet, cuddling her against his muscular, warm body. She turned her head and buried her face in between his pectorals and let go.

She cried for her loneliness and for her dead family and didn't stop there. She kept right on crying, getting all the fear and pain she had endured over recent days out of her system. God knew how long her jag lasted, but by the time her tears finally slowed down to the occasional hiccup, Jack's shirt was soaked where her head had rested.

And even though she knew she probably looked like something the cat had dragged in, she felt so much lighter, as if the weight of the world had lifted from her shoulders. At the same time, she was utterly exhausted. Her eyelids felt like they were swollen, and they burned from her binge.

Emma became aware of the silence in the room as she calmed. Jack hadn't said a thing since she had started crying. He hadn't tried to placate or stop her crying with meaningless platitudes. He had just continued to hold and support her.

"Do you feel better, sweetie?"

"Yeah." Emma drew in a ragged breath and finally sat up, wiping the moisture from her cheeks.

"Do you want to talk about it, Emma?"

"No."

"Okay, but if you change your mind you come to one of us. Okay?"

"Okay. I'm sorry I got your shirt all wet."

Jack cupped her face between his hands and then leaned in and placed a gentle kiss on her lips. "I'm not. You needed to get all that turmoil out of your system. You can cry on me anytime, Emma. Now, how about a nice, hot, relaxing bath?"

Emma pushed to her feet and headed toward the bathroom. She had been yearning for a bath or shower ever since she had woken up that morning. Her skin felt grungy, and she didn't think she would ever feel clean again.

"I'll take that as a yes, then." Jack followed her into the bathroom.

Emma was bent over the tub turning the faucets on when she felt Jack's presence behind her. She glanced over her shoulder to find his eyes glued to her ass. When he finally lifted his gaze to meet hers, she felt nearly singed by the heat that was in his eyes. Her breasts swelled and her pussy clenched, causing cream to drip out onto her panties. *Why did he follow me in here? Is he going to watch me bathe?*

Jack must have seen the question in her eyes because he began talking.

"I'm going to make sure you don't get those cuts wet, Emma."

"I'll be fine, Jack. You've already put the waterproof bandages on them."

Jack leaned back against the vanity, crossing his legs at the ankles and his arms over his muscular chest. His biceps bulged beneath the sleeve of his T-shirt, and the muscles in his abs rippled as he moved. Her breath caught in her throat and her heart rate escalated until she felt like she had just run a mile. How did these three men get to her so quickly? She'd never responded to such blatant masculinity or to such alpha men before. Why did her body have to sit up and take notice now?

"You realize we are Doms, don't you, Emma." It came out as more of a statement than a question.

"Yes, I know."

"When we have a woman in our bedroom we like to be called 'Master.'"

"Okay." Emma was totally perplexed because as far as she was concerned their sexual kink had nothing to do with her.

"How much experience have you had as a submissive, sweetie?"

Emma frowned at him, not sure where he was going, but she decided to answer him truthfully. "Um, none."

"That's what I thought. When a Dominant asks a question, he expects to be answered honestly and in full detail. A relationship between a Dom or Doms and a sub is based on trust."

"Okay. Why are you telling me all this?"

"Because you, little Emma, are a natural-born submissive, and the three of us would like to play with you."

Emma looked back at the tub and turned the water off. She didn't know what to say to Jack, so she didn't say anything at all. When she straightened and turned to face Jack, she became a little wary because all expression had left his face.

"Remove your clothes, Emma."

Emma fiddled with the button on the sleeveless shirt Charlie had lent her but didn't move to comply with his directive. Although she was attracted to Jack, as well as Tank and Gary, she didn't know them at all, and she wasn't used to being naked in the presence of a man.

"I can bathe by myself, Jack. I have been able to since I was a little girl."

A noise near the door drew her attention and she looked up to see Gary and Tank standing there looking at her. Gary frowned, but Tank's face was a mask of granite.

Gary stepped into the large bathroom and kept right on walking until he was standing in front of her with the tips of his shoes touching hers. "Emma, you were given an order. We expect you to do as you're told."

Emma tilted her head back so she could look Gary in the eye. The angle made the muscles in her neck ache, but she wasn't about to let these three men get away with telling her what to do. Not even if it was what her body wanted her to do.

If she was honest with herself, she wanted to strip her clothes off and let them touch her. Her body yearned to feel their hands and mouths caressing her all over. But after what she had been through at the hands of Andrew Mitchell, she was filled with trepidation. If she gave into them and gave them what she wanted—what she wanted, to feel them touching her all over—she was scared she would get hurt. Again!

"Look, I appreciate the fact that you are all trying to take care of me, but I don't need you to. I have been independent since I was a teenager. I know how to look after myself."

"That's not the point. Do you think we don't know you are attracted to us, Emma? Do you think we don't see when your nipples go hard and when you squeeze your legs together to ease the ache in that sweet-smelling pussy?"

And just like that her body began to react to his naughty words. Her nipples pebbled into hard, turgid peaks pushing against the cotton shirt. Her pussy clenched and her clit throbbed. Moisture gathered and then coated her folds only to drip onto her panties. She barely suppressed a moan as the image of these three men touching her, loving her, assailed her imagination. She wanted nothing more than to strip off, climb onto the bed in the other room and spread herself wide for theirs and her own delectation. Her mouth opened to plead with them to strip her naked and touch her but she couldn't bring herself to voice what she wanted. She snapped her mouth closed. Emma was shocked by the cravings which were tearing at her insides. The yearning was deep. Her body was aching and itching, and she knew that only these three men could put out the fire burning inside her. But she couldn't find the courage to speak of her need. She didn't really know these men and wasn't about to look like a fool for giving voice to her needs.

When she lowered her head to relieve the ache in her neck, Gary reached forward and grasped her waist, obviously taking pity on her. He lifted her up with ease, until she was on eye level with him. She placed her hands on his shoulders for balance. Having her feet and legs dangle wasn't very comfortable and she wanted to wrap her legs around his waist for further stability, but she wasn't sure she wanted to get that close to him, at least not yet.

"You are in our home, little one. When we give a command, we expect to be obeyed. *Immediately.* You can try to keep us at arm's length, but let me warn you that you will end up in our beds. If it wasn't for your injuries and the fact that you're still healing, you would be bent over one of our knees by now with a red ass." Gary lowered her until she was once more standing on her own two feet. He took a step back and then placed a finger beneath her chin until their gazes connected once more.

Oh God! Why does the thought of them spanking me turn me on? I should be running away after what I've just been through. She'd been alone and independent for so long and she coveted being free if only for a short while. The need to give up control had been a deep-seated longing she hadn't been aware of until she had met these three men.

Do I have the courage to let them take over? Can I trust them not to hurt me?

They hadn't hurt her yet. In fact, Gary, Tank, and Jack had gone out of their way to help her, treat her wounds, and keep her safe. She realized that she already trusted them with her body. If she hadn't she wouldn't be here in their house, but her heart was another matter.

"The only words I want to hear coming from that sexy mouth are, 'Yes, Master.' Now do as Jack told you and strip."

Emma shivered with sexual awareness. Gary's deep, firm, commanding voice caused shudders to race up and down her spine. She wanted to give in and obey that voice. They'd said she was a natural submissive, and maybe they were right. Her desire overcame her caution, and as she found herself slipping the buttons through the holes in her shirt, she murmured, "Yes, Master." When she had unclasped the last button, she shrugged it off her shoulders. The air in the room was cool and her nipples hardened even further, and her breasts ached for their touch. She kept her head lowered as she pulled the zipper on the skirt down and then wiggled and tugged until it was pooled around her feet on the tile floor.

"Good girl. Now remove your panties."

Emma did as he commanded. When she was standing naked in front of all three men, she felt vulnerable at being so exposed to them. And although she was exposed and defenseless, that vulnerability made her more aware of the men's power over her. Even though she was small in stature she'd never felt very feminine until now. Their sexual prowess and dominance turned her on like never before, but it was just physical. Her heart craved to be filled and if it turned out they were just using her, then she would at least have memories of their time together to look back on.

"You have a very sexy body, Emma. You have nothing to be ashamed of," Master Tank stated as he moved further into the bathroom. "Get into the tub, darlin', and we'll help you wash."

Emma stepped into the tub with Master Gary's help. He gripped her elbow and didn't release it until she sat down. Master Tank took a couple of steps back from the tub, and then, to her delighted surprise, he tugged his tight T-shirt up over his head and dropped it on the floor. She couldn't take her eyes off his hard, muscular physique. He was so brawny that his muscles flexed and rippled beneath his tanned skin with every movement. Emma wanted to crawl over to him and see if he was as hard as he looked.

Heat coursed through her body and swept up into her face as he continued to remove the rest of his clothes. Master Tank was the epitome of a Norse warrior. With his light hair and eyes and his Scandinavian ancestry, she could just imagine him standing at the prow of a ship calling to the oarsmen "stroke" as he captained the vessel. His large, solid thighs and lower legs would ripple as he stood with his legs apart to balance as the boat pushed through the water, riding up and down the waves. His shoulders were wider than any other man she had ever encountered, and his pecs were hard slabs that rippled and contracted each time he moved. His arms were stretched above his head and she wasn't sure if it was in a display for her or if he was easing kinks from his muscles. His torso tapered down to narrow hips with a slight line of hair from his belly button which led down to his groin.

Emma barely held in a gasp when she saw his cock. The man was seriously hung, and it wasn't even at full mast. She unconsciously licked her lips and watched with avid fascination as Master Tank's penis twitched and began to thicken and lengthen.

"Do you like what you see, little one?"

Emma closed her eyes and drew in a ragged breath. Her eyes opened quickly when she heard water rippling, and she exhaled shakily when her gaze connected with Master Tank's. He had stepped into the tub when she hadn't been looking and was now standing in front of her. His legs were spread shoulder-width apart, and he didn't seem to be worried that she could see him in all his naked glory. And what a glory that was. His balls hung down between his legs, big and heavy and darker in hue. His cock was now standing at full attention, and Emma had never seen a more magnificent sight. The tip of his hard cock was even with his navel, even though the shaft curved slightly to the right. The bulbous head was an angry-looking red-purple, and his shaft looked thicker than her wrist.

Master Gary's voice pulled her from her sexual trance. "Master Tank asked you a question, sub. When one of your Doms asks you something we expect to be answered honestly with no hesitation."

Question? What question?

Master Tank drew her gaze as he moved in closer. She let out a little squeak when he picked her up into his arms and then sat down where she had been sitting, placing her ass and upper thighs in his lap. Sitting sideways on his legs, she was facing Master Gary and Master

Jack but could still see Master Tank. Since she could now feel his humungous appendage pulsing against her hip and side where it was trapped between them, all she could think about was how big it was and what it would feel like sliding in and out of her pussy.

Emma wasn't used to being naked in front of anyone or having anyone standing naked in front of her. But what bugged her right at this moment—far more than the nudity issue—was what these three men wanted of her.

"Emma, you are trying my patience," Master Gary said coldly. "Did you or did you not like how Master Tank's body looked?"

Emma's brain finally kicked in. She felt annoyed by Master Gary's taciturn tone. "Oh for God's sake, he'd give Zeus a run for his money." She glared at Master Gary and then pinned Master Jack with a scowl.

Firm but gentle fingers gripped her chin, and she looked up into Master Tank's green eyes. He studied her face before he finally spoke. "What is it you want to say, Emma?"

"How do you..." Emma hesitated, not sure how to ask her question.

"No," Master Tank said. "Don't be shy with us, Emma." Releasing her chin, he cupped her cheek. "Ask what you need to, little one."

Emma tried to gather her thoughts, but it was a little difficult to concentrate when she was as naked as the day she was born and sitting in the lap of a handsome, sexy, naked man. Finally she got her brain in gear. "What do you want from me? Why are you doing this?"

Master Gary knelt down on the tiled floor and picked up a bath sponge. He squirted some gel onto it and began to wash her. Master Jack was leaning against the vanity watching the proceedings. There was enough heat in his eyes to boil her bathwater, but he seemed content to sit back and stay mute for the moment.

"We want a relationship with you, Emma," Master Tank said. "We've been waiting to share a sub between us for quite a few years now. You are exactly who we've been waiting for. You're the perfect sub to fit between the three of us, and we aren't about to let you go."

Emma squirmed on Master Tank's lap when Master Gary began to wash her breasts. Her nipples pebbled and her areolas tightened with need as he caressed the lightly abrasive sponge over her needy peaks.

"Hold still, sub," Master Gary commanded, and again, to her surprise, she froze.

"How do you do this to me?" Emma didn't even know she was going to voice that thought until she heard herself speak.

"You, my dear, little Emma, have a need to be controlled, and the fact that you trust us and are attracted to us lets you free yourself to obey our commands. We know you don't know us very well, and we still need to get to know you, but if you give us the chance we can show you more pleasure than you've ever experienced in your life. We all want you, Emma." Master Gary took a deep breath as he continued to wash her.

His hand was now between her thighs and inching its way up between her legs. She squeezed her knees together, halting his progress by trapping his hand and the sponge from going any higher.

Goose bumps formed on her skin, and her body felt like it was one big mass of need. Even in the warm bathwater, she could feel cream leaking out from her pussy. She ached to have his hands there, relieving the itch that had started when she first set eyes on the three men.

But she wasn't the sort of woman to jump into a relationship just because she was attracted to someone. Worse, she no longer knew whether to trust her judgment. She had known Andrew Mitchell for four weeks, and look what had happened.

But Master Gary was right. She trusted them with her body. She was curious to know what the attentions of three men would feel like, and she yearned to feel their hands on her. But she wasn't sure she trusted them with her heart. What if she jumped in with both feet only to get hurt?

She couldn't give herself to a man—or men—physically and not get emotionally involved. When she gave herself to someone, she did so wholeheartedly. Could she take the chance of getting her heart broken? The pain of the physical abuse she had suffered at the hands of Mitchell would be nothing compared to that.

Physical injuries healed. A broken heart didn't.

Chapter Six

We all want you, Emma. The words hung in the air like the steam from the bathwater. Gary kept his eyes on Emma, channeling patience as she processed what they'd told her. The yearning that passed over her face told him to spread her thighs on the spot, but in a matter of heartbeats her expression turned wary.

His heart sank. If Andrew Mitchell had broken her spirit, death was too good for him. Gary wanted to get to the caring, passionate woman hidden inside her. He wanted to bestow pleasure on her for a lifetime.

But if time was what she needed, as the trepidation on her face told him she did, he would take it one moment at a time. Pitching his voice low, he said, "Let us show you how good it can feel, Emma."

Her mouth firmed and she nodded with sudden resolve. Her voice, however, was soft and hesitant. "I want you, too."

Gary had never felt so proud of her. Although wounded, she was willing to fight. She'd stand up to them if she didn't like what they wanted or demanded of her, and she'd fight her own fear. She was absolutely perfect for them. She tugged at his heart like no other woman ever had, and he suspected that no other woman ever would. Little Emma was unique, and they intended to show her just how special she was.

Starting right now.

Gary nodded to Tank, knowing his friend would pick up on what he was about to do. Tank shifted Emma around on his lap so that her back was pressed to Tank's front and then he maneuvered closer to the side of the bath so that Gary could touch Emma without leaning over too far. She gripped Tank's forearms as if they were a lifeline, and his heart ached for this sweet, vulnerable woman. Tank lifted her arms up above her head and looped them around his neck. "Clasp your hands together behind my neck, darlin'. If you move them away, you will rack up punishments. Don't think we won't deliver whatever discipline you have coming once you're healed."

Emma did as Tank told her, and Gary separated her knees so that her legs were splayed wide and her feet hung over the outside of Master Tank's spread thighs. Gary washed Emma's pussy, being sure to caress the sponge over her little clit, but it wasn't enough. He needed to be able see her pussy unhindered by the water. He quickly finished washing her sex and then cleaned her ass. Once done he rinsed the sponge and lobbed it onto the side of the tub.

"She's clean. Let's get our sweet little sub out and dried off."

Jack had already snagged the clean towel that had been hanging on the rail, and when Tank handed Emma off to him, Gary once more lifted her arms above her head and clasped her wrists in one hand. Jack dried Emma quickly and Gary released her wrists and then picked her up, being careful not to touch the waterproof bandages on her back. He carried her into the bedroom and placed her in the middle of the bed with her ass on the end of the mattress. Jack was right behind him, and moments later Tank joined them after he'd dried off.

He couldn't wait another minute. Gary had to have a taste of her now.

Kneeling on the floor, he pushed her thighs apart and lowered his head toward her pussy. The sweet, musky scent of her arousal assailed his nostrils, and he inhaled deeply, taking her delectable aroma in. He bent down and swiped his tongue from the top of her slit down to her dripping hole and a little farther until he reached her ass. Emma moaned and her hips tilted as if offering him easier access to her sexy body.

Gary intended to have her writhing and begging him to make her come by the time he'd finished with her.

He licked back up to her pussy hole, stiffened his tongue, and thrust in as far as he could reach. The sounds she made warmed his heart, but their little sub was a wriggler. He lifted his head and found that Tank and Jack were half lying on the bed, their knees on the floor, their chests on the mattress, and their attention on Emma. Tank was devouring her mouth as if he was about to eat her whole, and Jack pinched one nipple while sucking on the other one.

"Hold her still," Gary said and then placed his mouth back in her honey-dripping cunt.

He flicked the tip of his tongue over her clit rapidly and smiled against her when she let out a small squeal and tried to shift away. Gary wrapped his arms around her upper thighs, which wedged his shoulders between her legs. He placed one hand on her pubic bone, and the other he splayed over her abdomen. Using the thumb of the hand on her pubis, he pulled the skin at the top of her slit taut, which made her engorged clit stand out even more. He laved it with his tongue.

He was aware of the squeals, whimpers, and sobs Emma made as he pleasured her, but he ignored them as he set about sending her over the edge into orgasm, comfortable in the fact that Jack and Tank wouldn't let her move too much and hurt her back. While he tended to her pussy, Jack and Tank alternately kissed her mouth and sucked on her nipples.

Gary removed the hand on her belly and caressed her anus before moving up to her pussy. First he pushed one finger into her tight, wet heat and eased it in as far as he could. As he withdrew, he turned his finger pad up and searched out her G-spot. He gave it a caress as he licked her clit, and she screamed with pleasure. Her cunt rippled around his finger and then released as she thrust her hips up toward his face. When he withdrew nearly all the way, he added another finger and pushed both back inside her honey-coated sheath, thrusting them in and out until she was on the very edge of climax. Then he changed his rhythm. Instead of pumping his fingers in and out of her cunt, he made little circles, making sure the pads of his fingers caressed across her G-spot. Gary counted in his head wondering if he would make it to five.

One, two, three...

She screamed the house down. Her vagina clenched and released around his fingers so hard, he wanted to bury his cock in her sweet little pussy and feel her sopping sheath squeezing him. He continued stroking over her hot spot and sucked her clit into his mouth, sending her over the edge again. His little sub didn't scream this time. She gasped and whimpered as if she had no breath left in her lungs, her body shaking and shuddering until she finally flopped back on the bed, totally replete and supine.

Gary withdrew his fingers from her vagina and licked up all her honey. When he was done, he lifted his head to stare at his beautiful little sub. Her cheeks were still pink from her climactic high, and her chest rose and fell rapidly as she gained her breath back while Jack and Tank soothed her with caresses to her arms and belly. She had closed her eyes, and he needed to see her.

"Open your eyes, Emma," Gary commanded, his voice deeper and more gravelly than usual with his arousal. He just hoped Emma wouldn't be frightened by the lust even he could hear in his own voice.

Her eyelids lifted, and he stared into her eyes, hazy with passion. He had never seen a more beautiful sight.

"That was so fucking hot. I can't wait to taste your little pussy, darlin'." Tank kissed her shoulder.

"I can't wait to sink into that pretty cunt from behind while I spank that gorgeous ass," Jack declared in a husky voice.

Emma threw an arm over her eyes and her cheeks went bright red. "Oh my God! I can't believe I let you do that."

"There is no need to be embarrassed, baby. You want us as much as we want you. Now, roll over so Jack can look at your back." Gary placed a hand on her hip and gently pushed her onto her side so she was facing Tank and with her back to Jack. The ends of the waterproof bandages had curled over, so they would need to be replaced.

Tank got off the bed and walked toward the bathroom. When he came back in, he was dressed and had the large first-aid kit from under the vanity as well as a damp washcloth. He placed the kit on the bed within Jack's reach and then he lifted one of Emma's legs and wiped her clean. When she protested and tried to move, Jack growled at her. "Don't move. I don't want to hurt you, sweetie."

When he was done, Tank and Gary watched as Jack removed the bandages.

"These are looking a lot better, Emma. I think it would be best to leave the bandages off for now. You can wear one of my T-shirts, which should be loose enough not to hurt you. Another couple of days and the wounds will nearly be gone." Jack finished up and helped Emma up off the bed. Tank had already retrieved a T-shirt, and Emma put it on.

"Okay, let's go downstairs and get some lunch. While we're eating we'll go over the rules."

She looked up at him, blinking in surprise as he took her hand. "The rules?" she repeated.

"If you want us to train you, you'd need to understand what we'll ask of you."

"Train?" she squeaked. "But I don't know—I'm not—"

Jack soothed her with a touch to her shoulder. "Let us explain first, and then you can decide. That's why we want to tell you the rules."

Gary all but saw her gather her courage. "Okay."

Gary led her from the room. Once in the kitchen he seated her at the table while he, Jack, and Tank saw to the food. Jack cooked the steaks while Tank got out a jug of sweet tea and glasses and brewed some coffee.

Once everything was ready and the coffeepot was full, the three men brought everything over to the table.

Gary placed a large steak on Emma's plate before putting it in front of her while Jack poured her coffee and added milk, just the way she liked it.

"Look, guys, I really think I should just head back home. I don't belong here and I need to get back to work."

Gary looked at Tank and Jack and saw the fear in their eyes. His gut was churning at her leaving before they had a chance to court her. He knew that if they let her go then their chance with her would be at an end, and that was something he couldn't live with. Nor was the fact that she would be in even more danger with Mitchell still at large.

"No," Gary stated with no inflection. Emma glared at him, but when he didn't bow to her play at dominance, she looked away. "Your life is in danger. I've already told you your boss doesn't expect you back at work until we've caught Mitchell. And what do you mean you don't belong here?"

"I live in a one-bedroom efficiency on the poor side of town. I don't belong in this neighborhood." Emma looked around the kitchen. Gary knew what she was seeing. The large, gourmet kitchen with state-of-the-art appliances. The quality tiles on the floor. The polished furniture in the dining room. "You guys are obviously comfortable financially." She swallowed audibly, looking anywhere but them.

"So you judge people by their material acquisitions?" Jack asked.

When she pushed her shoulders back and lifted her head, Gary knew she had found some of that internal fire. "What? No! How can you even ask me...I'm sorry, that didn't come out the way I meant it to."

"Yes it did. You don't feel comfortable because we have a nice house and things. You think we are too good for you, don't you, little one?"

Emma didn't answer Tank. She looked away and shrugged her shoulders.

"We aren't rich, Emma," Jack said and scrubbed his hand over his face. "Look at this from our point of view. We are three men with careers who happen to be best friends. Since we've known for quite a while that we wanted to share a woman, it only seemed natural that we pool our resources. We have three incomes coming into this house, so yes, we may have more money than some people. We don't judge you for how much you earn or where you live."

Emma frowned and lowered her eyelashes. "I'm sorry. I wasn't judging you. It's just that...I'm not used to being around nice things."

"Will us having more material things than you affect the way you feel about us?" Jack asked.

"No!"

"Then I don't see how it should matter."

"It doesn't. Sorry."

"Eat, Emma." Gary pointed toward her plate where her lunch sat untouched. "When we've finished, we'll talk more."

Jack began talking about the new equipment that was scheduled to be delivered to the hospital over the next couple of days. Gary knew his friend was taking their attention from Emma, and even though they all kept an eye on her as she ate, the tension left her shoulders now they were talking about everyday things. When she'd finished her salad and half the steak, she pushed the plate away and picked up her coffee. Gary knew she eaten her fill. It was time to explain their rules to her.

"Now you know we are Dominants, and you are a sub, one whom we'd like to have a relationship with. If you want to be *our* submissive, you need to know the rules." Gary held up his hand when Emma opened her mouth. "No, don't talk, just listen. When we're done explaining, you can ask your questions. Okay?"

"All right," Emma sighed and then waited expectantly.

"When we give you a command, we expect to be obeyed, and you are to answer whoever gave the order with 'Yes, Master.' We don't want you arguing or griping because you don't think you'd like what we want you to do. A good Dom will always push his sub's boundaries. You may think you don't want to do something, but we want you to try at least once.

"We would never do anything to cause you pain, but a Dom gives his sub what she needs. If he thinks a spanking is warranted, then he will spank her. But there is a difference between true pain and erotic pain. The slap of a hand or paddle on a sub's ass can drive her arousal higher than just plain vanilla sex and foreplay. In a scene a sub gives up all control to her Dom."

He noticed that her breathing had increased. Wide-eyed, she looked to Jack as he continued.

"We will tie you up and strap you down so you can't move, and then we will make you come over and over again. And when you don't think you'll be able to come again, we will wring one more out of you and then fuck you until you scream with pleasure." Jack glanced at Tank.

"Have you ever had anal sex, darlin'?" Tank asked.

"No," Emma answered and shifted in her seat. Gary looked down at her chest and saw that her nipples had just peaked into hard little buds. It seemed their little sub wasn't averse to anal play or sex. In fact, her body looked downright eager for it.

"The thought of having a cock up your ass excites you, doesn't it, Emma?" Gary asked, lifting his eyes to connect with hers.

"No."

"Don't you dare lie to me," Gary said in his cold Dom voice. He hid his smirk of satisfaction when Emma crossed her arms over her chest. He'd just bet that those hard nipples were throbbing for attention, and he watched as she moved her arm sideways as if trying to appease their ache.

"We've already told you that we would never hurt you."

"Your safety is the most important thing," Gary said. "You'll have a safe word. And of course, we'll make sure that asshole Andrew Mitchell can't get near you."

Whether or not she agreed to a relationship, he wasn't about to relent when it came to her staying here with them. The need to protect her was paramount.

Though he wasn't about to mention it now, Gary had a bad feeling about what Mitchell was doing. It seemed the asshole had vanished from the face of the Earth. There had been no cash withdrawals from his bank account and no purchases on any of his credit cards.

He was worried that Mitchell would bide his time until he could get his hands on Emma, once more. As far as Gary was concerned, that wouldn't happen, even if he had to give his life to prevent her from ever having to suffer at that fucker's hands again.

Emma had enough on her mind at the moment without thinking about Mitchell, though. Gary watched her lick her lips nervously. In a soft voice, she asked, "Will you make love with me again?"

There was nothing Gary wanted more. She had barely sampled what lovemaking would be like with him and his friends. But looking at the way she huddled in her chair, keeping her injured back from the wooden rungs, he knew it was too soon. They probably shouldn't even have touched her today, but Gary's brain had traveled south the moment he'd seen her gorgeous, sexy, naked body.

He didn't regret showing her what pleasure was like. His dick was still throbbing just from the memory of having her spread out on the bed. But he recognized now that they had to move slowly or she might try to run from them. "You're not ready." He held up a hand again when she opened her mouth to protest. He was pleased when she quieted at once. "You need to be trained first," he told her.

"You might like it, darlin," Tank said. "There's nothing in the world you have to worry about when you're with us."

Jack touched her hand again. "The training will be good for you, sweetie," he said.

Gary agreed. The structure of training would give her a way to process everything that had happened to her with Mitchell. If Emma was the submissive he believed she was, then she would feel truly safe when she let them take control. It would free her as nothing else in the world could after that abusive bastard's actions.

"You'll be under our power in every way," Gary said. He saw Emma tremble as the uncertainty in her eyes gave way to curiosity and desire. "Is that what you want?"

"Yes," she breathed.

Someday you'll be ours, little one. She was in their home, but that was only the first step. Now he just wanted her in his bed, by his side, and in his life. *Permanently.*

"Then let's get started," Gary said.

Chapter Seven

Emma dove into the water, delighting in its cool silkiness. She kicked the bottom of the pool and surfaced, smoothing her hair back from her face. It was a warm day for spring, and the sun had come out. The thought of cooling off while exercising had become very appealing, and not just because of the weather. Emma needed to expend some of her pent-up energy.

She started swimming laps, trying to focus on the feel of the water and not her frustrations. Whenever her mind was idle, though, it went back to her training sessions.

Training was nothing like she'd expected. She had to address each of the men properly, undress properly, stand and sit properly. Though she didn't understand why she enjoyed their attention, she did. It gave her a warm, fuzzy feeling to know she had pleased them. Whenever one of them told her to assume the "slave position," she felt as if her cares seemed inconsequential. To Emma that was a dangerous thing, but again and again she found herself obeying their every command.

Her frustration had nothing to do with training. Since the first night in their home, the three men hadn't touched her in a sexual way and Emma had no idea why. It wasn't that they weren't sexually attracted to her or that her presence when they were ordering her about didn't turn them on—she had seen the large bulges in their jeans when they were instructing her—but they were holding back.

She kicked off the wall of the pool, stroking harder. She wondered if they were waiting for something to happen. Emma certainly was. She was never totally relaxed. Though she loved the opportunity to live in the Doms' spacious, well-appointed house, she couldn't enjoy her leisure. Masters Gary, Jack, and Tank were adamant that she wouldn't set foot outside their house until Andrew Mitchell was behind bars for willfully holding her against her wishes and assaulting her.

Over the last few weeks she had never once been left alone in the house. Emma argued that she was a grown woman, but she was no match for the Doms in the debating department. They just crossed their arms over their chests, their feet spread shoulder width apart, and told her no.

So one of the Doms was always hovering somewhere. Masters Gary and Jack had to go to work, but she'd learned that Master Tank was a silent partner at the Club of Dominance. He'd made arrangements with Master Barry and Master Turner so that he could stay at the house and babysit her when the others were gone.

Right now, she expected that Master Tank was probably in his study still going over the accounts. A courier had called earlier in the day with papers for him from the club. The guy looked sort of familiar when Emma had taken the papers, but she couldn't quite place him. She'd delivered the papers to Tank and hadn't seen him since.

Fine by me. I need my space. Except Emma noticed herself looking for the men when they weren't with her. She missed the way they'd touch her arm or her back, the way they'd stroke her hair at the end of a training session.

Now if only she could get them to touch her the way she wanted.

After spending almost half an hour swimming from one end of the pool to the other, Emma's muscles were pleasantly tired. She stopped and rolled over onto her back and stared at the white, fluffy clouds. None of this would last forever, she knew, but the thought of leaving and never seeing her three Masters again wrenched her heart. When they were in Dom mode, they seemed cold and distant, but each had spent time with her and showed her their other sides.

Gary was such a hard-ass, but when he gave her a command in that cold, hard Dom voice, her body took notice. Her nipples pebbled and her pussy clenched, leaking cream as she remembered how the sound of his voice sent shivers up and down her spine.

She'd played chess with Jack nearly every night for the last week. Jack seemed to be the nurturer of the three men, but when he was in Dom mode he, too, became controlling and expected her to do as she was told.

Tank was a bit of an enigma to Emma. She had spent quite a bit of time alone with him and found that he wasn't much of a talker. He seemed to sit back and observe rather than integrate himself into a conversation, but she often found him watching her with his hungry eyes and a heated stare. Just a glance could bring her from calm and relaxed to blazing with arousal.

All three of them had indelibly worked their way into her heart. An ache formed in her chest and gathered in strength. Emma rubbed the spot over her heart and realized that she was deeply in love with three men. She didn't know how she was going to survive once she went back home.

Suddenly the water seemed more chilly than refreshing. She turned over and swam to the steps. As she dried off, the hair on her nape stood on end, and she looked toward the back fence. The property backed onto a lake, and although there was a fence surrounding the estate, except for the gate which led to the lake and small pier, she felt as if she was being watched. When she scanned the length of the tall sandstone wall and the wooden dock, as well as what she could see of the lake, she couldn't see anything.

God, Emma, now you're beginning to imagine things.

She headed inside to shower and dress. Master Tank was still hiding when she had finished, and Emma decided she would prepare dinner.

By the time she heard Masters Jack and Gary arrive home she'd made a potato salad and a tossed salad as well as a fruit platter, and the steaks had marinated and were ready to be grilled. She was just finishing up with the dishes when muscular arms wrapped around her waist and pulled her back against a warm, hard torso. She let out a small shriek of surprise and then looked up and over her shoulder into Master Tank's green eyes.

"Sorry, I didn't mean to frighten you, darlin'. I thought you heard me come in."

Emma's pounding heart settled a little, but her breathing increased when she felt the rigid bulge against her lower back. Masters Jack and Gary entered the kitchen. Master Gary went straight to the fridge and got out bottles of beer and handed them over to the other men.

"You've been busy, baby. Do you want a drink?" Master Gary asked.

Emma didn't usually drink alcohol, but today she decided she needed a little Dutch courage. She nodded her head.

She was sick of living in limbo. She intended to confront the three Doms tonight about returning home. If she couldn't be a part of their lives the way she wanted, she wouldn't stay.

Jack took a sip of his beer and leaned against the counter as Tank finally released her and walked around the other side to sit on a stool.

"How long before dinner is ready, sweetie?" Jack asked.

"Well, since I need one of you to grill the steaks it depends on when you want dinner. The salads are ready and we can eat as soon as the meat is cooked."

"I'll do that if you two want to get cleaned up before dinner," Tank said, but he hadn't taken his eyes off of her. He frowned as he took another swig of beer, and Emma did the same, wondering if she had somehow gotten food on her face while she had made the salads. The way he was looking at her, as if she was a bug under a microscope, was slightly disconcerting.

Emma decided she'd had enough of feeling uncomfortable and glared at Master Tank. "What?"

"Oh, sweetie, you don't want to be pulling the tiger's tail." Jack smirked before draining the contents of his bottle.

"What's on your mind, Emma?"

She just stared at Master Tank and then closed her mouth when she realized it was gaping open. "How do you do that?"

"You have very expressive eyes, baby. We know what you're thinking most of the time," Master Gary said as he walked toward her.

Emma's panties dampened at seeing him move with such predatory grace. Her nipples peaked and her pussy throbbed. She hoped they couldn't see how turned on she was, but from the heated looked he gave her, she didn't think she had succeeded in hiding her body's response to him.

"Do you know how fucking sexy you are, Emma?"

"Our little sub hasn't got a clue," Master Jack said as he rose to his feet and put the beer bottle into the recycle bin. "I think we should show her after dinner."

Emma ignored the byplay between Gary and Jack, though it made her heartbeat pick up. She was still hung up on how Tank knew she wanted to speak to them.

"I'm waiting, little sub."

She hesitated. If she asked Jack what he'd meant, maybe she would get somewhere with the three sexy Doms.

Oh, who am I kidding? They hadn't touched her since the first night staying in their house. She wouldn't put any stock in them making a move on her.

All of sudden she couldn't stand another moment of this. "I want to go home," Emma blurted.

The silence was pregnant as each of the men stared at her. She saw the way they all straightened and their muscles had tautened. Gary gripped her chin and tilted her head up until their gazes connected. "No."

Emma twisted her head, which displaced his hand. She backed up a few steps, until her waist connected with the edge of the sink, and she gave him a determined stare. "You can't keep me here if I don't want to stay."

Master Tank sighed as he moved closer. "Emma, it isn't safe for you to go home. That asshole probably knows where you live. Do you want to go through what happened before?"

"No." Emma's shoulders drooped but then she pushed them back again. "I hate living like this. I don't know how much longer I can continue to put my life on hold. I am going to lose my apartment. I can't afford to keep it if I'm not working and earning money to pay the rent."

"We'll take care of it," Gary said in a firm voice at the same time that Jack spoke.

"Then move in here."

"What?"

"Move in with us, baby." Gary placed his beer bottle on the counter.

Why do they want me to move in? Do they care for me? Don't get your hopes up, Emma. They're just being nice and don't want you to get hurt again.

"I can't do that. I can't expect you three to keep babysitting me indefinitely. It isn't fair to you."

"We like having you here with us, Emma. We don't want you to leave." Tank caressed the back of her hand.

"That settles it. I'll arrange everything." Gary stepped back and pulled his cell from his pocket.

Emma wasn't sure what he meant by "arranging everything," but she was sure it couldn't be good. Gary kept his gaze on her as he spoke into the phone.

"Mike, I need a favor. Can you arrange for one of your crew to pack up and move an apartment's worth of furniture?"

Emma stormed over to Gary and poked him in the chest. "What the hell do you think you're doing?"

Gary gripped her finger in his hand but ignored her as he continued speaking into the phone. Emma was so incensed at what he was doing she began to shake with fury.

"I don't fucking think so!" she raged and reached up to make a grab for the phone.

A large arm wrapped around her waist while a hand covered her mouth simultaneously. She was pulled away from Gary, but she wasn't about to let these three men control her life. Emma struggled and kicked out with her feet, but it didn't do her any good. Tank was too strong for her to escape from. She knew it was him by his unique scent of sandalwood and pine.

The more she struggled, the angrier she became. When he shifted his hold on her, he managed to pin her arms to her sides so she couldn't keep pushing at his arm. In that moment she felt so utterly female and controlled. Her body liked the sensation. Her pussy leaked cream onto her panties and her nipples elongated.

Jack moved to her front and grabbed her ankles as she tried to kick him away. He lifted her feet from the floor, and she hung between him and Tank. She twisted and turned, bucking and thrashing between them, but no matter what she did, she couldn't escape. Her eyes connected with Jack's. The heat she saw there made the embers inside her flare to a raging inferno.

Her anger morphed into a desire so deep, her pussy clenched and gushed out more of her juices. Her body ached. The need to feel their hands, mouths, and cocks loving her was more than she could stand. But the yearning in her heart for them to care for her, to love her emotionally as well as physically, was so profound that tears pooled in her eyes.

The two Doms carried her down the hall, to a room at the back of the house. She had seen the door and had tried to explore, but the entrance had been locked. She'd been curious about what was in the room but hadn't found the courage to ask.

Gary must have finished his call because he rushed around them and unlocked the door then held it open. She was carried inside, and she drew a ragged breath in through her nostrils when she saw what was in the room.

The room was large and filled with unconventional furniture. There was a St. Andrew's Cross in the center of the room. Off to either side were other weird-looking benches. Chains hung down near the far side. She glanced to her right as she was carried farther into the room and nearly moaned with excitement when she saw manacles on the wall which were on adjustable rails. It looked like the manacles would hold a person in place by the wrist and ankles.

But what drew her attention was the leather-covered stool-like seat secured to the wall. On top of the leather padding was some sort of…sex stimulator or dildo. At least that was what she thought it was.

Jack lowered her feet to the floor and then moved out of sight. Tank made sure she was steady on her feet before he released his hold on her. Footsteps sounded behind her, and she turned around to face Gary. Tank walked around her and stood next to Gary. All three Doms stared at her as if she was their last meal.

"Strip," Master Gary demanded in a firm voice.

Chapter Eight

Jack couldn't believe the fire burning in Emma's eyes. She had never looked so sexy. Her cheeks were flushed from exertion, her nipples were hard little points against the material of her T-shirt, and Jack caught the musky scent of her arousal.

He yearned to rip her clothes away and take her to the floor then bury himself balls-deep inside her petite little body. This, he sensed, was the real Emma. She submitted to them nicely when they were training her, but Dom/sub protocol had flown out the window as soon as she was mad, just as Jack had hoped it would.

She'd been meek with them when they taught her how to address them and how to assume the slave position, but she wasn't meek now. Jack and his friends had known that their little sub was full of passion.

Oh yes, little sub, you are perfect for us.

Now she stood before them with her chin thrust out aggressively, and although she was glaring at them, her lips were parted and her eyes were full of excitement. He wasn't worried that they would push her too far. When they had been training her, Gary had explained all about safe words and made her pick one. Each time they took her through what they would expect of her once they finally decided to play with her, they had always asked her to repeat it.

Emma crossed her arms over her chest and glared at them belligerently. It looked like their little sub wasn't in the mood to comply today. Jack mentally rubbed his hands together and thought, all the better.

"I gave you an order, little sub." Gary took a step forward, but Emma stood her ground. "If you don't start obeying me, you are going to rack up the punishments quickly."

"What is your safe word, Emma?" Tank asked.

"Chief." Emma practically spat the word.

Jack had nearly roared with laughter when Emma had chosen her safe word. He and the others knew it was her way of goading them since it was another word for Master.

"And how do you address us while we are in a scene with you, Emma?"

"*Master*," Emma replied facetiously.

"That's two." Gary took another step forward and nudged Emma's chin up. "You like it when we top you, don't you, Emma?"

"How do...How can I answer that? You've never topped me before."

"That's three."

"What? Why? What did I do?"

"You know very well what you did, Emma. Do you think we don't know that you like it when we top you? We haven't stopped mastering you since you arrived, and you love it, don't you, Emma, just like you love us?"

Emma tried to move her head away, but Gary cupped her cheeks between his hands. "Why are you so scared to admit that you care for us, baby? Is it because you don't think we care for you?"

Since she couldn't move away from Gary, the little minx closed her eyes and drew her lips into a tight line. Jack walked around Emma and came up behind her while Tank moved in close to her side. She was now surrounded by them, and they weren't leaving this room or letting her get away without answering them.

Jack landed a slap on her ass, and she gasped, her eyes flying open. It was time to set Emma straight and let her know how much they loved her. Jack and his friends had sat up after Emma had gone to bed the previous evening and planned out what they would do.

Since Gary was a detective and had a handle on reading people much better than he or Tank did, he had suggested pushing Emma's buttons by arranging for her stuff to be moved today. It seemed that his friend had read her right.

Although Jack and Tank also were more experienced at looking beneath the surface than the average person, and though they knew how to watch body language and decipher a sub's needs, Gary was more perceptive and comprehending.

Gary leaned down and licked over Emma's lips with his tongue, but their feisty little sub just pulled her lips in tighter. Jack was having none of that. He landed another slap on her ass, this time much harder than the last. He heard her gasp as the sting landed and smiled as Gary took advantage. His friend slanted his mouth over Emma's and devoured her. The little sobs and whimpers she made let him know she was turned on and involved in the kiss as much as Gary was. Jack groaned as she slipped her tongue into Gary's mouth. He pushed his hard cock into the small of her back and the top of her ass.

By the time the kiss ended, Gary and Emma were both breathing heavily. Jack couldn't wait another moment. He'd been patient for too long already. He reached around her waist, released the button, and lowered the zipper on her jeans, then pushed them down over her hips. Squatting behind her, he lifted her foot and removed one shoe and then the other. Once done he removed her jeans and panties. The sight of her delectable little peach of an ass called to him.

Jack kissed first one cheek and then the other, and then he kissed his way up her spine. As he had been removing her pants, Gary and Tank had stripped her shirt and bra off. There she stood in all her naked glory, and what a sexy, delightful little body she had. He couldn't wait until all three of them were making love to her at the same time.

By the end of the scene Emma would know how they felt about her, and he hoped she wouldn't want to leave.

* * * *

Tank's cock and balls were aching so much he was in danger of shooting off in his pants. As a Dom that was the last thing he wanted to happen. It was all about control and seeing to their sub's needs first. At a nod from Gary, Tank swept Emma from her feet and carried her over to the St. Andrew's Cross. As he lowered her to her feet and positioned her body, he leant down and kissed her. He'd never tasted a woman so sweet, and he knew he would never get enough of her. He thrust his tongue into her mouth and slid it along hers. Her little whimpers and moans grabbed at his heart and wouldn't let go. By the time he slowed the kiss and lifted his head, Jack and Gary had her secured to the cross.

Emma's face was tinged pink with desire and excitement, her arms and legs secured to the cross and spread wide open for them. Her full breasts were high and perky on her chest, and her hard little nipples were a dusky rose color, filled with blood and need. He perused her body and nearly moaned out loud when he saw the dew glistening on her bare, puffy, pink lips.

Tank knelt down at her feet and ran his fingers through her slit. Their sub was so turned on, her juices were running down her thighs. He stroked her pussy from clit to ass and back again, but he wanted to see how she tasted. Bending forward, her placed his mouth close to her pussy and lightly blew. She rewarded him with a long moan.

Oh yes, our little sub needs this as much as we do.

Tank moved the last couple of inches and thrust his tongue into her pussy. Her sweet and tangy essence exploded on his tongue, and he decided then and there that he wanted to have more of her cum in his mouth. He looked up when movement off to either side of her caught his gaze, and he watched Gary devour her mouth with his while pinching one turgid peak as Jack sucked on her other nipple. Closing his eyes, he concentrated on giving Emma the pleasure and love she deserved.

Tank withdrew his tongue from her pussy and sucked her labial lips into his mouth, cleaning her of her juices and swallowing them down, but it still wasn't enough. He wanted, needed more. He licked his way up her slit with the tip of his tongue and flicked it rapidly back and forth over her clit. She bucked her hips into his face and cried out.

"Yes, little one, that's it. Give Master Tank your pleasure," Gary panted after he lifted his mouth from Emma's.

Tank eased a finger into her cunt and slowly pumped it in and out, giving her time to get used to the feel of him penetrating her. He kept his eyes on her belly and watched it jump and tremble with each rasp of his tongue and thrust of his finger, but it still wasn't enough.

He wanted her screaming as she climaxed. Adding another finger to her pussy, he stroked in and out, and with each pass he made sure he caressed her G-spot. When her sheath rippled around his fingers, he knew she was getting close to orgasm. Opening his mouth wide over her clit, he sucked her small pearl into his mouth and gently held it with his teeth. He flicked the tip of his tongue back and forth over her engorged nub and tapped against her sweet spot.

Emma screamed. Her pussy clamped down on his fingers so hard he could barely move them, but not once did he let up as she bucked and trembled in the throes of climax. She yelled and whimpered, her sheath contracting, and cream gushed out around his digits until finally the last ripple faded away.

Tank gently removed his fingers from her cunt and then sucked and licked up all her cum. Then he kissed her thighs and belly as he caressed her legs. Jack and Gary were both running their hands over her body as they eased her down from her climax. He rose to his feet and leaned his forehead against hers.

"Do you think that if we didn't love you, we would see to your pleasure, Emma?"

"Y–You l–love me?"

"Yes, darlin'. I love you so goddamn much I hurt with it. Why do you think we want you here where we can keep you safe?"

"I–I…"

Tank stared into her moisture-filled eyes and kissed her. He hoped his kiss showed just how much she meant to him. When he once more lifted his head, tears were running down her face. With Jack and Gary's help they released the restraints around her ankles and wrists and he picked her up and then carried her across the room to the sofa. He sat down with her on his lap and surrounded her with his arms.

"Shh, Emma, everything will work out. Just let us in, darlin'. We have so much love to give you. All you have to do is let go."

* * * *

Emma didn't know why she was crying but she couldn't stop. When Master Tank had told her he loved her, the ache in her chest had eased, and now she was so full of emotion she was overflowing. Then she realized that he'd said "we."

Does that mean that they all love me? No, how could they?

She wasn't anything special. She felt connected to these three men in ways she had never felt to another human being before. She wanted to say the words back, but she just couldn't bring herself to open up like that. Everyone she'd ever cared about had left her, and she wasn't going to put herself out only to have her heart shattered into a million pieces.

She'd never thought such pleasure had existed, and they had only touched her with their hands and mouths. What would it be like when they eventually made love with her? Emma knew that they would end up having sex. It was as inevitable as night turning into day. And she wanted that more than anything. Her tears finally stopped, and she felt safe, warm, and secure in Master Tank's arms. She had never felt so cherished in her life.

"Feeling better, little sub?" Master Gary asked.

Emma sat up and wiped the tears from her face. She gave Master Gary a nod and then looked to over to see Master Jack smirking at her.

What is his problem?

"Oh, you are just racking up the punishments, aren't you, little sub?"

Emma frowned at Master Gary but quickly wiped it from her face when he looked at her sternly.

"That's three, Emma." Master Gary reached down and lifted her from Master Tank's lap. "How do you address a Dom, Emma?"

Oh, shit. Emma had forgotten to answer him verbally and had just nodded. She lowered her eyes, even though it was hard to do when she was in his arms, and replied in the sweetest voice she could muster. "Yes, Master Gary."

"Now, that is so much nicer. Don't you think so?"

"Yes, Master Gary."

"And do you know why I arranged for your lease to be broken and to have your things brought here?"

"No, Master."

"Are you sure, Emma?"

"Um. Maybe because you care for me?"

"I don't just care for you, Emma. I love you, baby. And I will do everything within my power to keep you safe."

Emma's breath hitched in her throat, and she looked up to see Master Gary watching her. As she looked at him, his eyes seemed to blaze with the love and affection he had just voiced to her. Moisture filled her eyes but she didn't let the tears fall. She blinked rapidly to dispel them. He kissed her lightly on the lips and then lowered her to her feet. When she was steady he placed his hands on her shoulders and turned her to face a low bench.

"I want you on that bench, Emma. Put your hands on the sides and your hips level with the edge."

Emma didn't hesitate to do as she was told. The bench was made of padded leather and was thin enough that her breasts hung on either side. The end was slightly raised, which tilted her hips and ass up. Master Jack came over and cuffed one wrist while Master Tank secured the other. Master Gary stood behind her and gently spread her thighs apart, and then she felt thick straps wrap around her upper legs. Fingers ran underneath the cuffs, checking to make sure they weren't too tight and wouldn't cut off her circulation.

She was comfortable in a strange way with her knees on the padding below the bench. She felt cherished as they made sure she wouldn't get hurt and also open and vulnerable at the same time. When she was tethered, Master Jack knelt down so she could see his face through the hole in the bench where her head was resting.

"Are you comfortable, sweetie?" Jack asked.

"Yes, Master."

"That's a good little sub." Master Gary stroked her back. "What's your safe word, little one?"

"Chief."

"Good girl. I love you, sweetie." Jack stroked a finger over her lips and then he got to his feet again.

Emma waited with bated breath. Her muscles tightened as she wondered what they were going to do to her, although she had a pretty good idea, since she was on what appeared to be a spanking bench with her ass tilted up in the air.

Smack.

She gasped as a large hand landed on her flesh. The pain was minimal, but the sting and heat which followed traveled to her pussy, causing more of her juices to leak out and her clit to ache.

Smack, smack, smack.

The three slaps alternated from one butt cheek to the other, never landing in the same place. Then the globes of her ass were being massaged and caressed, and she felt the heat from the sting spreading.

Another *smack* landed, and this time the hand remained where it had landed, holding the heat into her skin.

"You're doing real good, baby. You're taking your punishment like a good little sub should." Master Gary's voice sounded a lot deeper and huskier than normal, telling Emma that he was just as turned on as she was. "Five more, Emma, and then we're done."

Smack.

Shivers raced up her spine as the sting on her ass morphed into tingles of pleasure.

Smack.

Her clit throbbed and she tried to push her hips back, but she was held fast.

Smack.

Her butt cheek wobbled, and pleasure caused her pussy walls to ripple.

Smack.

She drew in a deep breath as her heart stuttered and her breath hitched in her throat.

Smack.

Emma sobbed and wiggled her hips when her pussy clenched and more fluid leaked from her vagina to coat her thighs.

Oh God. Please. Please just give me one more smack so I can come.

She jerked and then moaned when fingers caressed up and down her slit. They explored all the crevices and valleys but didn't penetrate her or touch her clit like she needed them to.

"So fucking wet." Master Gary finally tapped on her clit, but the quick touch wasn't enough. "A good sub needs to be rewarded. Let's get her loose."

Hands worked on her wrists and thighs, and moments later she was free to move. She stayed still, not wanting to piss her Doms off, which would probably lead to another punishment.

Wait! Since when did I start thinking about them as mine? Oh, shit. Why did I have to go and fall in love with them?

One of them wrapped his arms around her waist, and then she was lifted from the bench and up into Master Gary's arms. He carried her to the wall near the door, where there was a large chaise lounge that she hadn't noticed before. He sat down, taking her with him until her tender ass connected with his denim-clad thighs. Master Gary tilted her face up, and then his mouth was on hers.

Emma mewled as he swept his tongue into her mouth. He ate at her as if he were starving and couldn't get enough. The kiss they shared was hot, wet, and carnal, and it had her so aroused she yearned for them to make love to her all at the same time. When they were both breathless he lifted his head and stared deeply into her eyes.

"Will you let us love you, Emma? We all want to be with you at the same time."

Emma didn't have to stop and think about her answer. She replied with a resounding, "Yes!"

Chapter Nine

One moment Emma was sitting on Master Gary's lap, and the next he was carrying her from their play room. He took her upstairs to the large bedroom she had been sleeping in. That surprised her. Emma had expected her three Doms to make love with her in what they referred to as their dungeon, but it seemed they had other plans.

Once inside her room, Master Gary lowered her to the bed, and then he arranged her limbs so that she was lying in the middle of the mattress in what she would describe as a star position. She was spread wide open with her head resting on a pillow. Master Gary gave her a stern look.

"Do not move, Emma. If you do you will earn another punishment."

"Yes, Master Gary."

Master Gary gave her a pleased smile and then he moved to the end of the bed. Masters Tank and Jack stood there and looked over her body with so much heat and hunger, she felt the fire down to the tips of her toes.

Master Tank was the first to move. He pulled his T-shirt off and threw it to the floor before taking his hands to the waist of his jeans. Emma didn't know where to look first. All three men were shucking their clothes as if they had a time constraint. She unconsciously licked her lips and stared at the flesh which was revealed. They were such handsome, sexy men. Emma's body responded to them as they undressed, and when they stood before her totally naked, the urge to touch and kiss them all over was nearly too great. She was just about to move, but Master Gary gave her a hard look and she was able to remain still. At least for now.

Master Tank was so muscular that he literally bulged everywhere. Her eyes ran down from his wide shoulders, over his pumped-up pecs, to his ripped abs, his narrow hips, and strong muscular thighs, to finally linger on his large, engorged cock. He was so damn thick and long she wondered how his big cock would ever fit inside her much smaller body.

Emma shifted her gaze to Master Jack. He was a lot leaner than the other two men, but no less impressive. His shoulders weren't as wide as Master Tank's with his leaner athletic physique, but he was ripped and taut and absolutely perfect in her eyes. His hand moved up and down his hard, long shaft, and Emma wanted to crawl over to the end of the bed and taste the drop of fluid she could see glistening on the end of his penis. She once more licked her lips, trying to imagine what his pre-cum would taste like.

Master Gary groaned and stepped toward the bed. Emma gasped as her eyes ran up and down his impressive, masculine body. Damn, he had some muscles on him. He wasn't as tall or beefy as Master Tank, though there was only a slight difference in their sizes. His cock wasn't as long as Master Jack's and not quite as thick as Master Tank's, but somewhere in between. Emma felt a shiver of trepidation run up and down her spine.

How the hell am I going to take all three of those at once?

Master Gary must have seen her concern. "We would never hurt you, Emma. I promise we will go slowly with you. If you don't like anything we do and want us to stop, just use your safe word, baby. If you're unsure and need a break I want you to use the word 'yellow.' Okay?"

"Yes, Master Gary."

"Such a good little sub." Master Tank skirted around the end of the bed and climbed on next to her, and Master Jack did the same on her other side. Master Gary got up on the end of the bed and watched her as he sat back on his haunches between her splayed thighs.

"We need to prepare your ass, baby? Do you have any objections to anal sex?"

"No, Master Gary."

"Have you ever given head before, sweetie?" Master Jack asked.

"Um, once, Master Jack, but I don't think I was very good at it." Emma felt heat rise in her face, but she still answered honestly. The last thing she needed to do was lie and end up earning herself another punishment, although she had really liked it when she was being spanked. She would have to make sure she pushed her Doms' buttons at a later date. She wanted to have their hands and mouths on her whenever she could. The thought of being smacked on the ass for a grievance and then being brought to orgasm after accepting her punishment caused her pussy to clench and cream to leak onto her thighs and ass.

"Why would you think that?" Master Gary frowned at her.

"Well, the man I did it to, didn't um…You know."

"No, Emma, I don't know. You are going to have to tell me."

Emma knew by the twinkle in Master Gary's eyes that he knew damn well what she was talking about, but it seemed he was determined to make her say the words. She narrowed her eyes and nearly frowned at him but caught herself in time. "I didn't make him blow," she said, and then hastily added, "Master Gary."

"You're learning, little one. You please us all very much." Master Gary placed his large hands on the tops of her thighs and smoothed them up and down her skin. Tendrils of heat spread from her thighs to her pussy and up over her belly to her breasts, which made her nipples harden.

Master Jack cupped her cheek and turned her head toward him. She barely had the time to take a breath before he covered her mouth with his. Emma moaned into his as his tongue slid along hers and tickled the roof of her mouth.

Warm lips encased one of her nipples, and then a wet tongue laved over the turgid peak. Master Tank then sucked the little pebble into his mouth and suckled hard enough to cause her a slight pain. But the pain was so pleasurable that she pushed her chest up into his mouth, needing more of the sensations he bestowed on her.

A sharp slap landed on her thigh. "Don't move, Emma," Master Gary growled in his deep voice. She sobbed with relief when his hands finally got within an inch of her mound, but then, to her frustration, he didn't move any higher. It seemed like he was in the mood to make her wait. Emma didn't know if she would be able to handle such sweet torture.

Master Jack lifted his head and began to lick and nibble his way down her neck until he reached her other nipple, sucking it into his mouth. The sensations of having three handsome, sexy Doms touching her was almost more than she could stand, but she needed so much more from them.

The passing minutes seemed like hours as they played with her body, but Master Gary still hadn't touched her where she needed it most. Juices continuously dripped from her aching pussy, and Emma was just about to scream at him to touch her. She opened her mouth and drew in a ragged breath to do just that, but before she could make her demands, his fingers spread her pussy lips and then his mouth was upon her.

Master Gary licked and sucked, but not once did he touch her throbbing clit. Emma sobbed and felt moisture on her cheeks. She didn't even realize she was crying until she felt the tears tracking down her face.

"How much longer are you going to hold back from us, Emma?" Master Gary asked after lifting his head.

Emma frowned at him because she had no idea what he was talking about.

"Please." She tilted her pelvis up, begging him to ease the ache inside her.

"You've just earned another punishment, little sub," he said in his Dom voice.

Emma had had enough of their teasing. She needed some relief and she wanted it now.

"Oh God, I can't stand any more. Please?"

"Please what, Emma?"

"Please make me come."

"Not until I think you've earned it," Master Gary said. He thrust a finger up into her sheath. He pumped it in and out a few times and then withdrew again.

Emma kicked out, and her foot connected with his chest. That bastard didn't even grunt, but he captured her ankle in a firm grip. He nodded to Masters Jack and Tank, and they restrained her. She hadn't even realized that there were restraints attached to the bed, but her ankles and wrists were cuffed, and no matter how hard she tried, she couldn't get free.

"You are going to give us what we want, Emma. You can fight us all you like, but we will win in the end." Master Gary wrapped his arms around her thighs and lowered his head and laved his tongue over her needy little nub.

She tried to push her hips up, but two more sets of hands landed on her body and held her still. Master Gary thrust his fingers into her cunt, and Emma cried out at the carnality of the act. Her insides were on fire, and only these three men could put out the flames. Just as she felt her internal muscles contract, Master Gary lifted his head and pulled his fingers from her pussy.

"Why?" Emma cried. "Why are you torturing me?"

"We aren't torturing you, Emma, we're loving you." Master Gary caressed her inner thighs. "We'll give you what you need when you give us what we want."

"I don't know what you want."

"Yes you do, darlin'." Master Tank leaned down and kissed her on the lips.

She knew that Master Gary wasn't about to let her come until he had what he wanted. The yearning to have them make love to her was monumental, and she wanted to know what it was like to be loved by three men. More than that, she wanted them to know how she truly felt.

Emma drew in a ragged breath and closed her eyes. Could she really give them what they wanted? If she opened herself up to them and they walked away, she would be alone again. Could she deal with the heartache if that happened?

If they could put themselves out there and tell her they loved her, why couldn't she? Hadn't they taken a risk by telling her how they felt? Damn, she was such a coward. It was time to grab hold of life and hang on. Emma hadn't been living. She had been existing. She had already taken the first step into life by going out with Andrew Mitchell, and even though she had ended up hurt, she had also found love and security with her three Doms.

She inhaled deeply, opened her eyes, and looked at each man in turn. "I love you. I love all of you so much, it hurts."

Emma lowered her eyes when they didn't say anything, and she began to feel uncomfortable. She felt so exposed and wanted to cover her naked body as well as hide her heart back behind the walls she had let down. Tears filled her eyes, and one trickled down her cheek. Just when she was about to lose control of her emotions, gentle hands tipped her face back up. Masters Gary, Jack, and Tank each looked at her and let her see what was in their own hearts.

"Don't ever doubt that we love you, Emma." Master Gary caressed her face with his fingers. "We've known how you felt about us for a while. We could see it in your eyes, baby. I know how hard it was for you to say that, and I thank you from the bottom of my heart. Please don't put those walls back up around your heart. You need to let us in so we can show you how much we care for you."

"You are such a brave little sub." Master Tank stroked her shoulder and down her arm. "I love you, Emma. Please, don't ever think I don't. You have filled my life with such joy and happiness."

"You are every breath I take, little one." Master Jack smoothed a hand over her belly. "Without you, my life has no meaning. You've given me so much to look forward to. I know how hard it was for you to declare your love for us. We understand that you were hurt when your family was killed. But please, don't hide your heart away from us like you have been doing from everyone else. We love you, sweetie."

Emma's chest began to ache. She was so full of love and happiness that she didn't know if she could contain the emotions. It had been so long since she had been held and loved. She missed her parents and sister, but she knew they wouldn't want her hiding away from the chance of a lifetime. They would want her to leap in with both feet and hold on to the wonderful chance she had been given.

She felt hands at her ankles and wrists, and moments later she was released from the restraints. Master Gary lifted her into his lap and cradled her against his warm, muscular chest.

"Shh, baby, don't cry. We'll never let you go, Emma. You are our entire world, little sub."

Emma hadn't realized she was crying until Master Gary mentioned it. She wrapped her arms around his waist, held on tight, and let go. She cried for all the lonely years she had endured and for the death of her family, and then her sad tears turned to tears of happiness. Who would have thought that she would find the loves of her life after being held against her will and assaulted?

Master Gary just held her until her tears were spent. When they finally slowed she became aware of Masters Jack and Tank rubbing their hands on her back and arms, offering her comfort. Emma gave Master Gary a final squeeze and then lifted her head from his chest and wiped the moisture from her eyes and face. She laughed when she saw she had made Master Gary's chest wet with her tears and swiped her hand between his pecs to remove the dampness.

"I'm sorry for getting you all wet."

"I'm not." Master Gary kissed her lightly on the lips. "Do you feel better, baby?"

Emma thought about it before answering. She actually did feel better. She was so much lighter, as if the weight of the world had lifted from her shoulders.

"Yes. I do. Thank you for holding me." She looked into Master Gary's eyes and then turned her head to see Masters Tank and Jack. "Thank you for offering me comfort. I think I needed to let go of all the baggage I was carrying around in my heart. You all telling me you loved me started to break down the ice I had enclosed my emotions in."

"We'll always be here for you, sweetie." Master Jack lifted her from Master Gary's lap and walked toward the bathroom. "How about a shower before we continue with this? I think the warm water will help you relax even more."

"Yes, that would be nice."

Master Jack helped her in the shower, and she did feel much better. He wouldn't let her walk back into the bedroom. He picked her up with the ease of a strong man and carried her back to the bed.

Master Tank was lying on the bed and Master Gary was sitting on the small sofa against the far wall, talking quietly to his friend, but they stopped their conversation when Jack and Emma entered. They looked so damn sexy with their muscular bodies on display, and Emma felt her arousal begin to simmer again.

"Emma, we think our first time together shouldn't be with us as Doms and you as a sub." Master Tank sat up and shifted until his back was against the headboard of the bed. "We want to make love with you and show you how much you mean to us, how much we love you, and how much pleasure we can give you. Will you let us do that for you, darlin'?"

Chapter Ten

Jack handed Emma off to Tank, and he cradled her on his lap. She wiggled and squirmed when she felt his thick, semihard cock begin to pulse and twitch as it filled with blood once more. Her pussy clenched and juices leaked out to cover her labia and dribble down onto her ass.

"Oh yeah, our woman likes that idea." Tank lifted her up and turned her around so that she was straddling his hips and thighs. "She's dripping so much she got me wet."

Emma moaned when Tank shifted her so that his cock was against her pussy. When he shoved his hips forward, his erection slipped between her lower lips and nudged against her clit.

"Fuck yeah, darlin', your pussy is so hot and wet. I can't wait to get inside you."

Tank reached up and fisted her hair. He pulled her face down to his and kissed her rapaciously. Emma sobbed and whimpered as his tongue danced with hers, and she began to rock her pelvis. His hard rod slid through her wet folds, and with every forward move, the tip of his cock caressed her engorged little pearl.

Tank released her mouth, and she was glad she wasn't the only one who was left panting for breath.

"I can't wait much longer, Emma. I need to be inside you."

Tank grasped her hips and lifted her until the corona of his cock kissed the entrance to her pussy. He kept her pinned with his gaze and slowly began to lower her onto his monstrous dick. Emma mewled as he first penetrated her body. He was so big, her body resisted.

"I need some help," Tank rasped as he looked over her shoulder.

The bed dipped to either side of her as Jack and Gary climbed onto the bed with them. Gary moved behind her and clasped her ribs to hold her steady. Tank kept one hand on her hip, and the other moved down to her mound. He caressed her sensitive skin, and then one of his fingers found her clit and began to make light circles over the aching bud.

Emma cried out as pleasure swamped her, and she wondered how she would endure so much ecstasy. He wasn't even inside her pussy yet, and already she was in danger of climaxing. The two men held her steady between them, and then Tank pushed up against her. The wide head of his cock popped through her delicate flesh, and he held still, waiting for her to adjust to his intrusion. The pleasure-pain of being penetrated and stretched by his thick crown was such sweet agony and she wanted more. She wanted to feel him buried deep inside her cunt. She lifted up, wiggled her hips, and pushed down, moaning as his cock gained more depth.

"Don't move, baby. Let us do all the work." Gary kissed down her neck and across her shoulder.

Jack reached over and pinched a nipple between thumb and finger. Little zings of electricity sparked down from her breast to her clit, causing her pussy to clench and release more juices.

"Shit, she likes what you're doing." Tank gasped. "Keep it up. She's covering me in her cream."

Tank withdrew his hand from her pussy and gripped her hips again. He held her still and began to thrust his pelvis up and down. Emma groaned as with each movement of his hips Tank's cock forged his way inside her. She'd never felt such rapture and she never wanted it to end.

"You are so fucking tight, Emma. God, you feel like heaven and home." Tank looked over her shoulder at Gary and then kissed her lips. He maneuvered down the bed until he was lying almost flat. He wrapped an arm around her waist and pulled her down just as a hand on her back nudged her forward with a gentle push.

Her pussy pulsed and rippled with excitement, but her head wasn't sure she was ready to love three men at once. Gary must have seen her muscles tense up because he rubbed a hand up and down her back. "Just remember, if we do anything that is too much or you don't like it, use your safe word, baby. If you say 'yellow,' we will stop and talk about what the problem is, but if you say 'chief,' then everything stops. Okay?"

"Okay."

"Don't forget that we love you, sweetie." Jack leaned down and kissed her mouth. "We would never want to cause you unnecessary pain."

Emma took a deep breath and exhaled slowly, willing her muscles to relax so that she wouldn't hinder Gary. She just hoped that she would enjoy what was about to happen and not freeze up. The need to have her three men loving her at the same time negated her uncertainty.

"A little cold, baby," Gary warned just before lube drizzled down the crack of her ass. Emma shivered, but it was with excitement rather than trepidation. "Try and stay relaxed for me, Emma. I need to stretch you out before I can fuck this sexy little ass."

She moaned when Gary massaged the lube into her anus. Her vagina clamped down on the thick, hard cock buried in her pussy. Had she known how good it was to have her asshole touched, she might have tried it a lot sooner. Gary took his time with her and didn't force his way into her back hole. He rimmed her back entrance with his fingers until her muscles relaxed and she felt her anus open to him.

"Yeah, you like that, don't you, baby? You like me touching your pucker."

"Yes. God, please. I need more."

"I'll give you more, Emma. I can't go too fast or I'll hurt you. Take a few deep breaths, sugar."

Emma did as Gary told her and let her body go lax on top of Tank while she concentrated on keep her breathing even and deep. She felt her muscles relax even more, and then she sobbed when Gary pushed a finger into her ass. He moved his finger from side to side, stretching her and coating her insides with lube. She gasped when he withdrew his digit from her body, but then he was back with two fingers that were coated with more of the cold gel. By the time he had three fingers deeply embedded in her dark hole, Emma was one big, aching mass of need.

"She's ready. Hold her tight so she can't move." Gary was breathing heavily and his voice was much deeper than normal.

Emma whimpered when Gary pushed his lubed cock against her rosette. He held her hips firmly so she couldn't move, but his grip didn't hurt her. Her anus spread, and she moaned as pleasure and pain mixed together. The burning pain only seemed to heighten her desire, and she tried to push back against him.

"Don't move, baby." It sounded like Gary was talking through clenched teeth.

The head of his cock popped through the first ring of muscle, and he held still. One of his hands released her hip and moved up to caress her back. "Good girl, Emma. Your ass is so fucking tight. You're squeezing me tighter than a fist."

Gary pulled back slightly, and then he pressed forward. With each inch his cock gained inside her ass, he stopped and waited, giving her time to adjust to his penetration. When she finally felt his balls connect with her flesh, Emma's insides were on fire. She needed relief after waiting for them to make love with her for so long. Juices dripped from her pussy in a continuous stream. Never had she felt such need before.

Tank fisted her hair and tilted her mouth up to his. He kissed her hard and fast, and then he and Gary helped her to sit up between them. Movement off to the side caught her attention, and her eyes snagged on Jack's hand as he stroked it up and down his long, hard cock. He was on his knees close to her side, and Emma licked her lips as she wondered what the drop of pre-cum glistening on the tip would taste like.

"Do you want some of this, sweetie?" Jack asked as he fisted his cock near the head.

Emma didn't answer. She was too enthralled at seeing his hand on his dick to reply so instead she leaned over and licked around the bulbous head of his cock and dipped her tongue into the slit.

"Oh, fuck, Emma, lick me some more." Jack moved his hand down to the base of his cock.

Emma laved her tongue all over and around the crown of his dick, and then she opened her mouth and sucked him in. Jack groaned but he didn't thrust his hips forward. He stayed still and let her take what she wanted. She moved her mouth up and down his cock until she got into a nice, steady rhythm, and when she pulled back to the top, she made sure to rub the spot underneath where the head met the shaft. Jack's moaning and groaning let her know he was enjoying what she did to him.

Just as she got comfortable, Tank and Gary began to move inside her. Tank held on to her ribs and Gary her hips. As Tank thrust forward, caressing her internal walls with his hard cock, Gary withdrew from her ass to the tip of his penis. With each advance and retreat, they picked up the pace incrementally until their bodies slapped against hers as they plunged to the hilt inside her.

Her pussy rippled, and her blood heated until her bones felt like they were liquefying with bliss. Jack reached out and tugged on her hair. "Sweetie, I'm getting close. Pull off if you don't want to swallow."

Emma wanted all of him, needed to feel and taste his essence as he came in her mouth. She cupped his balls, and this time when she sucked him in, she pushed forward until she felt his tip reach the back of her throat.

Breathing deeply through her nose, she was able to control her gag reflex and then took him down even further. She gently rolled his balls and swallowed around the head of his cock. Jack shouted as his dick expanded, and then he was shooting ropes of cum into her mouth and throat. Emma swallowed rapidly, drinking his slightly salty jism into her body. When he was done and his cock began to soften, Jack eased from her mouth and stroked her face. He kissed her forehead and then flopped down onto the bed.

"That was fantastic, sweetie. Your mouth feels like heaven."

Emma smiled, but then mewled with delight and closed her eyes as Tank surged into her sheath. Her womb felt heavy, and her internal muscles coiled tighter and tighter. Gary pressed into her bottom when Tank retreated. The blissful sensations which were centered at her pussy expanded and covered her entire body. Her muscles began to quiver and shudder, and she felt like she was about to explode.

"Oh, you have to stop, it's too much."

"No. Don't you dare fucking fight it, Emma. Let go and come." Gary panted and nipped her shoulder.

The pleasure was so intense Emma didn't know if she would survive. Jack pinched one of her nipples just as Tank slid a hand down to the top of her slit. The spring inside her snapped, and she screamed as wave upon wave of euphoria consumed her.

Cream gushed from her pussy, covering Tank's cock and her inner thighs. Tank and Gary pumped into her hard and fast so that they were both filling her at the same time. Another wave of rapture washed over her as one orgasm turned into two and more fluid seeped from her vagina. Pinpricks of light formed before her eyes, and Emma gave herself over into the care of her men.

She was only vaguely aware of Tank and Gary shouting out their releases. First Tank yelled, and one thrust later Gary roared with gratification. She was totally boneless and slumped down on top of Tank.

Her eyelids were too heavy, so she gave up and let them close. Hands caressed and soothed her, and as her breathing slowed with her heartbeat, she drifted down into sleep.

* * * *

Gary gently eased his cock from Emma's ass and went into the bathroom to clean up. When he came back into the room, he helped Tank lift her off him and settled her on the bed. He lifted her leg and cleaned her ass and pussy and then Jack gently dried her off. Just as he was about to get into bed, his cell phone rang. He rushed over to his pants and retrieved his phone from his pocket, answering as he stepped out into the hall so he wouldn't disturb Emma.

"Hi, Turner, what's up?"

"That asshole Mitchell turned up here and was harassing Aurora. Since she was the only one on the desk at the time, he tried to beat her up."

"Fuck! Is she all right?"

"Yes, but she has a black eye. The prick got away before we could get to him. Mike chased him, but Mitchell had too much of a head start. He was on a dirt bike and after he left the grounds he headed off-road."

"Shit." Gary sighed with frustration. "Do you want me to send Jack over to check on Aurora?"

"No. She's okay. Mike is tending her. Of course she's being stubborn, but between him and his brother, Mac, going Dom on her, she doesn't stand a chance."

"I'm glad she's all right. What did Mitchell want? Was he looking for Emma?"

"Aurora doesn't think so. Before Mike showed up, he was yelling 'I know where she is.' Aurora thinks he was frustrated that he couldn't get to Emma."

"So he's lashing out at others connected to the club," Gary finished. He could hear the worry in his own voice. This couldn't be allowed to happen again.

"Is Emma safe at your place?"

"There's no way the asshole's getting past our security. If he's figured out that Emma's here, he's probably in the neighborhood." He considered arranging for some uniformed officers to drive by regularly, but he was beginning to think they needed to take action. "Thanks for the heads-up, Turner, and please give my best to Aurora."

"I will. Don't hesitate to call if you need help. You may want to think about staying here for a while. At least there'll be more of us around to help out if things come to a head."

"Let me talk it over with Jack and Tank. I'll get back to you."

Gary ended the call and entered the bedroom. Jack and Gary were cuddled up next to Emma, but each of them looked up when he returned. He nodded toward the door and then headed for the kitchen, knowing his friends would follow shortly. Coffee was brewing in the pot by the time they came down dressed in their jeans. When they each had a cup of the dark brew, they sat down at the table, and he explained what Turner had told him about Mitchell.

By the time they had finished discussing the best way to catch the fucker, it was nearly two in the morning. They headed to back to bed with Emma, but it was a long time before Gary was able to close his eyes. His mind was racing as he thought about what they would ask of Emma in the morning. He only hoped they weren't putting her in even more danger.

Chapter Eleven

Emma knew something was wrong as soon as she entered the kitchen. She'd awoken in bed not long ago to find that Gary and Jack had left the room. She had been draped all over Tank, who had been stroking her back and squeezing her ass when she'd opened her eyes. She had loved waking up in his arms but had missed Jack and Gary. Now that they had told her they loved her and she had finally opened up and reciprocated, she needed to have them close. Their relationship was still too new, and she didn't like waking up without all of her men by her side.

Tank had helped her to shower and then to dress, and now she wondered if Jack and Gary had been talking about her when she walked into the kitchen, because they had gone quiet when she entered.

Tank guided her to the table and then got her a mug of coffee. Jack and Gary finished up cooking breakfast and then served the food. Emma didn't feel very hungry when she looked down at the scrambled eggs and toast, but when she caught Gary staring at her, she knew he would kick up a fuss if she didn't eat at least some of the food. So she picked up her fork and began to eat. She was only able to eat half the food since it had been piled high. When she was done she pushed her plate away and wrapped her hands around her mug of coffee.

"Sweetie, there's been a bit of a problem in regards to Andrew Mitchell." Jack placed his hand on her thigh and gently massaged the muscle, which had tensed up.

"What did he do?"

"He got into the club and assaulted Aurora." Gary scooted his chair back from the table and pulled her from her seat and into his lap when she gasped.

"Oh my God. That fucking asshole. Is she okay?"

"Two Doms from the club are taking care of her."

"Aurora thinks Mitchell knows where you are," Gary said.

No. I'll have to leave. The thought so filled Emma with panic that she couldn't speak. Gary continued soothingly, "He won't get to you here. He can't get past our security."

She remembered something she'd almost forgotten. "Yesterday I think I saw him. Well, I didn't see him." She shivered, recalling the sensation of being watched by eyes beyond the fence. "But I think he was there."

"You're safe, sweetie," Jack said.

"But Aurora wasn't!" Emma sat up straight. "What happens if Andrew tries to hurt someone else at the club?"

The men exchanged a glance.

"Baby, we think we may have a way to capture this asshole and put him behind bars." Gary tilted her head back so he could see her eyes.

"What do you want me to do?"

Gary inhaled deeply and wrapped his arms around her waist, hugging her tight. "If you are too scared, we'll understand."

"What Gary is trying to say is, will you let us use you as bait?"

Emma opened her mouth to begin asking questions, but Gary interrupted her. "I want you to hear us out and know everything before you answer, baby. What we want to do is make it seem like we've left you alone. Of course we would never do that, but we want Mitchell to think you are vulnerable. There will be officers hiding nearby, and we will be, too."

"Where do you want to do this?" Emma questioned.

"We may have to make it look like you're alone a couple of times." Tank sighed and ran a hand through his hair. "We were talking last night and this morning. We have every reason to believe he's watching the house, so if he sees you leave the house alone he'll follow your car.

"One of us will hide in the backseat of your car. We've all been in the military, we're Marines, so we know how to protect you, darlin'."

"At the club, we'll need you to stand in the parking lot for a few minutes. We'll make it look like the area is clear, but there will be officers in unmarked cars all around you. If he sees you standing alone and vulnerable in the parking lot, the bait will be irresistible."

"Why not wait until I'm in the club?" Emma asked.

"After what he did to Aurora, I doubt the coward will be brave enough to come back," Tank said with a growl.

"Even so," Gary said, "Masters Barry and Turner will make sure that someone is watching the security cameras at the club at all times, and those men will have our cell phone numbers set on speed dial so they can call us if we're not with you."

"What if he doesn't take the bait?" Emma asked. "What will happen then?"

"Then we will spend a pleasurable night showing you the world of Dominants and submissives. Do you trust us to take care of you, sweetie?" Jack reached over and clasped her hand in his.

"Yes. I trust you three more than I have ever trusted anyone in my life."

"Thank you, baby. You have no idea how much that means to us. Let us explain about the club."

"There are rules to adhere to, and you will have to sign a contract just like every Dom and sub who enters the doors to the Club of Dominance. But the most important thing you need to know is that the motto of the club is always safe, sane, and consensual." Tank paused to take a sip of coffee.

"There are monitors throughout the club who keep an eye on the scenes being played out. If at any time you want to halt proceedings, then all you have to do is use your safe word. Whenever a new sub enters the club, the monitors are informed of that sub's safe word before play begins."

"I don't want to be whipped," Emma blurted out. "I don't want to feel that sort of pain again. Plus I'm scared that if Mitchell gets hold of me he won't stop until he's killed me."

"Oh, baby, we would never do that to you. We already know you aren't into pain. The most we would do to you would be taking a flogger to you or our hands." Gary tugged her other hand and pulled her into his lap. "And there is no way we will let Mitchell anywhere near you."

Emma felt comforted and safe when she was in the arms of one of her men, and she sighed with relief at his answer.

"Wait. What's a flogger?"

Gary rubbed her back in soothing circles. "A flogger has tendrils of soft leather or suede. The only thing you would feel would be light stinging."

Emma tensed.

"Don't be scared, sweetie." Jack ran his hand over her hair. "We think you would enjoy that slight pain, but if you're not sure, all you have to do is use the word 'yellow,' and we'll stop and talk to you. If you don't like it, then just use your safe word and everything stops."

Emma nodded at Tank and then looked into Gary's eyes as he began to speak again. "Do you know what subspace is, Emma?"

"Subspace?"

"Subspace is when the sub is so full of endorphins they go into a sort of a trance, like they're floating on a cloud. They are only aware of their own bodies and Doms and nothing else. A good Dom will feel a rush of desire and heightened awareness as he tops his sub while sending him or her into subspace. It's a rush for all concerned."

After all their talk Emma was horny and wanted to go back upstairs with her men for the rest of the day, but she had to know everything that was going to happen so she would be safe in case Mitchell showed up.

"I think you like that idea, don't you, Emma?" Gary's deep voice drew her attention.

Since she knew she couldn't hide her body's reaction from these three men because they watched her avidly most of the time, she didn't bother to hide her arousal.

"Yeah, I do."

"Such a good little sub," Jack praised.

"How do you feel about being naked in front of other people?" Tank asked.

Emma shuddered again and closed her eyes as heat permeated her cheeks. The thought of being exposed to others filled her with trepidation as well as desire.

"The thought excites you and makes you nervous," Gary said. "Just remember we would never leave you alone inside the club, and no one but us will ever touch you. We will push your boundaries, Emma, but we won't do anything that is a hard limit for you. We've already ascertained you aren't into sadomasochism or hard pain, and neither are we for that matter."

Emma shivered but this time with revulsion. No, she wasn't into pain and she was glad her men weren't either. The thought of going through what Andrew Mitchell had dealt out to her again made her feel sick to the stomach.

Gary cupped her chin and looked into her eyes. "Don't worry so much, baby. We would never inflict pain on you."

"I know," Emma sighed and leaned her head on his shoulder. "I trust you all to know what I need."

"We can't ask for anything more than that, sweetie. We promise to take good care of you." Jack stroked a finger down her arm.

"I want you to rest today, darlin'. I need to contact Masters Turner and Barry and make sure all the monitors know your safe word and are aware you are to be protected the whole time we are at the club. After dinner tonight, we will go to the club." Tank rose to his feet and began to gather the dishes.

When Emma stood to help, Gary snagged her around the waist and pulled her back onto his lap. "Since Jack is shorter than Gary and I, he will hide in the back of your car. I'll give you the GPS from my truck and I'll program it to show you the route I want you to take. There will be an unmarked police car trailing you and a few others on the side of the road at strategic places. You will be safe, baby. We aren't about to take any chances with your life."

Emma shifted on Gary's lap and wrapped her arms around his neck. "Thank you. I just hope that Mitchell takes the bait. I hate the thought of having to look over my shoulder constantly. The sooner he gets caught the better." As tired as she was of living in hiding, she felt a pang of doubt. None of them had mentioned the order to have her furniture sent here. They seemed to have forgotten about her moving in with them. What if Mitchell was caught and they expected her to just go back home? Emma stood up, too anxious about everything to stay still a moment longer. "I'm going to help Tank clean up the kitchen."

She gave Gary a kiss and then headed over to help Tank.

"I have to go into the precinct for a while to make sure everything is ready for tonight but I'll be home for dinner." Gary gave Emma a smile and then left.

"I have to make a couple of calls." Jack walked over and hugged Emma from behind. "After you've finished here why don't you go and watch a movie or read for a while? Do you remember how to work the entertainment system?"

"Yes."

He kissed her on the temple and left the kitchen.

As Emma and Tank worked, they talked.

"I know you are all retired Marines," Emma said. "But how did you all meet?"

"We were in the Middle East for nearly a year." Tank handed her the rinsed plate so she could put it in the dishwasher. "Gary and I were in the same team so we were already friends. We were caught by a band of insurgents and were under heavy fire for nearly three days. We were lucky that we weren't killed."

He was staring out the kitchen window but Emma knew he wasn't seeing the backyard. He was lost in his memories.

"A couple of our men were wounded, and by the time backup arrived, our commanding officer, Keith, had also been shot. We managed to get out and get our wounded help. Jack was the medic who treated our comrades and CO. If it hadn't been for Jack our commander would have died. We visited Keith every day and got to know Jack real well. We just sort of clicked and became great friends. We haven't looked back since."

"Did all your friends survive?" Emma asked and rubbed a hand on Tank's back.

"Yeah, darlin', they did. We were lucky."

"I'm glad."

"Me, too, darlin'. Me, too." He kissed her lightly on the lips.

They finished cleaning up in companionable silence. Once done they headed for the living room. Emma had decided a movie would be better for now because she didn't think she would be able to concentrate on reading. Her mind was in turmoil over what was to come tonight, and not just the part about luring Andrew Mitchell to make a move.

She was excited about going to the club and having her three men play with her. Emma had no idea how she was going to get through the day. She only hoped that she would get to play out a scene with her three Doms. The thought of being totally exposed for anyone to see turned her on, and she craved to have her men touching her, torturing her with pleasure until she begged them to make her come.

It had been such a surprise to learn that she was submissive. After spending years being independent and looking after herself, Emma would never have dreamed that giving up control in the bedroom or anywhere else in regards to sex would be so rewarding and freeing.

She'd only had one session of play with Gary, Tank, and Jack, but she craved so much more. Even though she was excited to find out more about herself and her Doms, she was also apprehensive.

What if something went wrong and Andrew Mitchell managed to get hold of her? Would she ever get the chance to experience the world of true submissiveness with her guys? What if they weren't happy with her level of submission? Would they still want to be with her?

Emma still had so many unanswered questions, and she just hoped she would be enough for them. She pushed that thought aside, because she trusted them to never really hurt her. After all, they had been so angry at what Mitchell had done to her and had taken good care of her as she healed.

Emma got comfortable and tried to concentrate on the movie as it began to play, and she prayed that nothing would go wrong tonight. What if Andrew hurt her men in trying to get to her? She couldn't stand the thought of them getting hurt because of her. But the most frightening thought of all was what would happen if he succeeded in getting hold of her.

Will he kill me this time?

Chapter Twelve

Her hand shook as she brushed her hair and looked in the mirror. Her face was so pale she looked ill. She nearly dropped the brush when she placed it on the counter. Leaning over she braced herself and tried to stay composed. Emma was so nervous her stomach was churning. In a short time she would be driving toward the Club of Dominance. Her legs felt like soggy noodles and she wondered if her shakiness was visible. She took a few deep breaths trying to calm her anxiety and then opened the bathroom door and entered her bedroom. Gary was sitting on the bed waiting for her.

"Hey, baby, are you all right?"

"Yeah, just a bit nervous."

"You have nothing to be scared of, Emma. We'll make sure you're safe." Gary rose to his feet and pulled her into an embrace. She felt so secure and warm in his arms that she never wanted to leave.

"I have an outfit I want you to wear tonight."

"What?" Emma asked with a frown.

"There's a dress code at the club. All subs have to wear corsets, bustiers, or nothing at all. I don't think you're ready for the latter."

"No, me neither." Emma stepped out of Gary's arms and eyed the outfit on the bed. It consisted of a deep purple leather miniskirt and a black corset. There was also a pair of *fuck me* shoes on the floor. She eyed the heel and wondered how the hell she was going to wear those all night long. Emma wasn't used to such high shoes and hoped she didn't twist her ankle as she walked in them.

"You don't have to wear those shoes for long, baby. It's up to the sub and her Dom, or in your case Doms, but most of the time subs go barefoot inside the club.

"I have already set up the GPS in your car and set the route. Why don't you get dressed and be down in the garage in ten minutes? Tank and I are leaving now. We will meet you at the club. Jack is already downstairs, hiding in the backseat. No one will know he's there. Just try to relax and act as if nothing is wrong, baby. If you look too nervous and that asshole is watching, he may suspect something. Don't worry about watching your rearview mirror. I have a couple of police officers who will take turns tailing you to the club.

"When you arrive at the club, I want you to pull up out front and wait there for a few minutes. We'll already have officers in unmarked cars in the parking lot. If Mitchell shows himself, they'll move in."

"If not?" she asked hopefully.

"Then head inside. Master Mike is on valet duty. He'll take your car around back so Jack can get out without being seen. If Mitchell follows but doesn't reveal himself, there's no point showing him that it was a trap he didn't fall for. Jack will come in the back way. Do you have any questions, Emma?"

"No."

"All right, I'd better move. I'll see you there, baby." Gary gave her a last hug and then kissed her before he released her and headed out.

Emma watched Gary's ass flex behind his black denim jeans until he was out of sight. She loved that her men didn't dress up in leather but were comfortable enough with their dominant masculinity to wear their jeans and tight T-shirts. It seemed to her that they were each comfortable with their dominance and had no need to put it on display. They were masculinity personified and, thank you, God, they were all hers.

Emma dressed, brushed her hair once more, and then put on light makeup. Anxiety had made her pale, but a light sweep of blush to her cheeks added a little color. With one last look in the mirror, she turned away and stepped into the shoes and headed downstairs.

Masters Tank and Gary had already left. Emma got into her car, inhaled deeply, and turned on the ignition. She pressed the button to open the automatic garage door and backed out. She was so nervous that when she changed gears, she put the stick in third instead of second and nearly stalled her car. When a warm hand brushed against her hip, she jumped.

"Everything is going to be fine, sweetie. Don't talk to me in case that asshole is watching. Try and relax, Emma. We will do everything we can to keep you safe."

Some of the tension left Emma. Knowing Jack was with her every step of the way was reassuring.

The twenty-minute drive seemed to take forever, but she finally pulled her car to a stop near the front steps to the club. The front of the building was deserted. Emma got out of the car slowly, bracing herself for another vehicle to pull in behind her and Andrew to jump out. She reminded herself that Jack was in the backseat and there were officers in the lot. She scanned the parked cars, wondering where they were, before remembering that she should try to act as if nothing was out of the ordinary. For want of anything better to do, she tinkered with the straps of her high heels.

No one drove up after her. After a few minutes of heart-pounding waiting, the door to the club opened. A tall, muscular man came down the steps. He was as big as Master Tank in height and bulk but he looked like a real bad-ass. *This must be Master Mike. God, I'm so glad he's not my Dom.* The aura of power emanating off of him was enough to send any woman running whether they were submissive or not. She pitied any sub he came in contact with.

He opened her door before she could and held out a hand toward her. Emma took his hand and let him help her from her car.

"Hi, Emma, I'm Master Mike. If you ever need anything, honey, just give a yell. Okay?"

She looked over her shoulder at the silent parking lot. *I guess he didn't take the bait.* She didn't know whether to feel relieved or disappointed. "Thanks," she said distractedly to Master Mike.

Emma looked up into the lightest blue eyes she had ever seen. A shiver of trepidation washed over her and shivered up her spine. He was frowning at her and those eyes had gone ice cold.

"You're heading for a spanking, little sub. Don't think I won't speak to your Doms," Master Mike said in a cold, gravelly voice.

Shit! I forgot to address him correctly. Emma lowered her eyes and apologized. "I'm sorry, Master Mike. Please, forgive my lapse?"

"Very pretty, Emma. Now go on and head inside. Master Barry has some papers ready for you to fill out."

Emma rushed around the front of her car and up the steps, careful not to turn her ankle in the stiletto heels she was wearing. She looked over her shoulder as Master Mike drove her car around the far side of the club. Releasing another deep breath slowly, she stepped over the threshold of the club's entrance. Now that she was inside she felt more of the tension seep away. It helped to see Charlie's smiling face as she neared the reception desk in the foyer. There was another petite, blonde-haired woman who had a black eye, standing next to Charlie. Emma knew this had to be Aurora, the woman who had taken a beating from Mitchell because of her. Aurora was talking to some other people, but she smiled in greeting and Master Barry nodded his head to her.

After Charlie and Master Barry explained all the rules, protocols, and policies, Emma filled out the paperwork. She handed the pages back when she was done.

"Give me your shoes, Emma," Master Barry demanded. "Your Doms want you barefoot."

She bent down and removed her shoes and then handed them over to Master Barry. He passed them to Aurora, who placed them out of sight under the counter.

"I'm sorry you got hurt because of me, Aurora." She looked the other woman in the face.

"Don't be silly. It's not your fault, honey. You can't control what assholes will do."

"Thank you," Emma sighed as the guilt she felt waned. She was grateful that the receptionist didn't hold her responsible for getting hurt.

"Okay, let me just clarify what your safe word is, Emma," Master Barry said as he skirted the end of the reception desk.

"Chief."

"And why did you pick that word to use?" Barry asked as he and Charlie guided her toward the double doors to the inner sanctum of the BDSM world.

"Umm, I–I…"

"Let me guess. You wanted to piss off your Doms." Master Barry looked down at her and smiled.

Emma smiled back cheekily. "Yes, Sir, I did."

"Oh, Emma, I like you already. You and I are going to be great friends." Charlie laughed.

Master Barry's face changed from amused to blank in the blink of an eye as he turned toward Charlie. "Did I give you permission to speak?"

"No, Master Barry. Sorry, Master Barry."

Emma lowered her head to hide the smirk on her face. Charlie hadn't stopped smiling and she began to shift from foot to foot as Master Barry stared at her. It looked like the voluptuous beauty was turned on by the tone of her husband/Dom's voice.

Barry turned away from Charlie and opened the doors. As he did, Emma caught Charlie sticking her tongue out at Master Barry and had to bite her own tongue so she wouldn't burst out laughing.

As she followed Master Barry, she looked around surreptitiously from beneath her eyelashes. It was like she had walked into another world. The last time she had walked through the great room it had been empty. Now the sights and sounds caused her to shiver with nervous excitement. Women cried out in pleasurable pain and climax as their Doms took them through their paces and catered to their needs.

She caught sight of a male sub on the St. Andrew's Cross, where his female Domme spanked his bare ass with what looked like a paddle of some sort. The dance floor in the middle of the room was nearly full with bodies swaying to the music. There were a lot of subs dressed like her, but there were also some who were totally naked. But from what she could see, no one leered and everyone seemed comfortable with nudity. On the stage off to the other side of the dance floor, a female sub was cuffed to a chain and her ankles were shackled to hooks in the floor. She was spread open for her Dom as he fucked her with a dildo or vibrator.

Charlie halted when Master Barry stopped at the bar on the far side of the room. She looked up to see Masters Gary and Tank watching her as she approached. Master Gary crooked his finger at her making a *come here* motion, and Emma walked around Charlie until she was standing next to his stool. Master Tank leaned against the bar next to him.

"Yes, Master?"

"Very nice, Emma." Master Gary snagged her around the waist and pulled her between his spread thighs. "Mike already called and gave us a report. It seems Mitchell won't be drawn out of hiding that easily."

"We'll catch him, darlin'," Tank assured her. "Maybe not tonight, but soon."

"Did you have any trouble on your drive?"

"No, Master."

"I'm glad to hear it."

"Are you ready to get started, little sub?" Master Tank asked, drawing her gaze.

"Yes, Master Tank."

"Such a pretty little sub." Master Tank straightened and clasped her hand, then began to lead her toward the stage where the sub and Dom were just finishing up. The Dom had placed a blanket around his sub's body and was carrying her down the steps. Another woman wiped the chains down, cleaning them. Emma stopped walking when Master Tank turned toward her. He stared at her with a blank expression.

"Take your clothes off, Emma."

Emma wanted to argue that she didn't feel comfortable being naked in front of so many strange people, but when she looked into Master Tank's eyes she knew if she opened her mouth she would be in big trouble. Her hands trembled when she reached up to release the first hook from its eye at the top of her corset. By the time she had reached the last one, her legs were shaking. The corset fell from her body, and she caught it before it hit the floor.

"Such pretty breasts you have, Emma. Look at those hard nipples," Master Gary said from behind her. She could feel heat emanating from his big, hard body and knew if she leaned back, they would touch. "Now remove your skirt."

Another shudder traveled her spine as she took off her skirt. She was totally naked and felt very vulnerable, but she was also aroused. Her pussy clenched and cream leaked out onto her thighs.

"Looks like I'm just in time," Master Jack said as he stopped near her side. His heated eyes traversed her body, causing another shiver.

Master Gary walked around her until he was standing next to Master Tank. He was holding something in his hand, but he whipped it behind his back before she could ascertain what it was. "Give me your hands, Emma."

She held her hands out toward him and he had her wrists cuffed before she could blink.

"Such an obedient little sub. You're doing great, baby." Master Gary hooked the cuffs together in front of her and then grabbed hold of the short chain between her wrists. He led her up the steps of the stage. Masters Tank and Jack followed.

He halted when she was standing beneath the chain, and he raised her arms above her head.

Moments later, Emma was restrained by her wrist and ankles. She was surrounded by her three Doms, and although she felt safe, she was aware of all the other eyes on her naked body. Her nipples elongated even more and her clit throbbed with need.

Master Gary walked around behind her and ran his hands over every inch of her body. His hands caressed from the top of her head to the tips of her toes. "You like being on display, don't you, sub?"

"Yes, Master."

"I'm glad you didn't lie to me, Emma. I would have known if you had lied to me. Your body lets me know what you're feeling." Master Gary ran his fingers through her wet pussy and down her damp inner thighs. "I'm going to cover your eyes, Emma. That way you can't be distracted by the people watching and your senses will be heightened."

That was the only warning Emma got. Cloth covered her eyes and then she was totally blind. A large, muscular arm wrapped around her midsection and then one of them licked over her lips. She inhaled deeply and knew it was Master Tank in front of her. Emma gasped and then moaned as Master Tank kissed her hungrily. By the time he drew away, Emma was so aroused she was close to climaxing.

A sharp slap landed on her ass, drawing her back from the brink. Each time the hand connected with her ass cheeks, the sting radiated out and into her pussy. With each smack the force of the slaps escalated and Emma thought she may have to use one of her safe words. If she said the word *yellow* then they would stop and she could gain control over her impending orgasm, but if she did she would only earn more punishment. Just as she was about to speak, someone's warm lips sucked one of her nipples into their mouth. She sobbed as the stinging pain to her ass morphed into pleasure. Another mouth sucked her on her other nipple, and Emma cried out as shivers of adrenaline and arousal permeated her body. Her mind was confused, and she didn't know at first if she was feeling pain or pleasure. Then she realized that she was feeling both, but the pleasure far outweighed the pain. A whimper of frustration escaped her mouth when the smacks to her ass stopped and the two men at her breasts released her nipples with a pop.

Just one more smack. Please? One more smack will send me over the edge.

Emma felt a breeze, which told her that her men were moving. She wanted to be able to see what they were doing but then wondered if she would be able to let go if her eyes weren't covered. No, she didn't think so. Master Gary had known that she would feel more comfortable with her eyes covered.

How does he read me so well? Even I didn't know that until just now.

The air in front of her stirred again, and something soft was rubbed over her body. She inhaled and knew by the lemony scent that Master Jack was at her front. He rubbed whatever he had in his hand over her neck, shoulders, breasts, and down her belly. Emma arched her hips forward and then gasped when a hard slap landed over the middle of her ass.

"Don't move again, sub," Master Gary ordered in a deep voice.

Emma held still but it was a lot harder than she imagined. Her instincts were to arch up and rub her needy body against Master Jack. She sighed when the soft thing caressed her pussy lips and moved between her legs, but she bit her tongue to keep in her growl of frustration when it was removed.

A light flick landed on her thigh. Emma felt the impact in several places, and her pussy clenched with the desire to be filled. She had no idea what Master Jack was using on her, but it felt so good. The taps came at her faster and harder. Master Jack covered her body from her breasts down to her inner thighs. Her breasts were so swollen and her nipples so achy that she needed their hands on her to relieve their sensitivity. Her clit throbbed and her pussy leaked out her juices in what felt like a continuous stream. She wanted one of her men to fuck her hard and fast until she screamed with orgasm, but they were in control and wouldn't give her any relief until they were ready.

Emma didn't know how much more she could take. She was on the verge of an orgasm so big it was scary, but Master Jack wouldn't hit her where she needed him to.

"Please, Master?"

"Please what, little sub?" Master Jack asked in a breathless voice.

"Please, can I come, Master Jack?"

"Just a bit longer, sub. What are your safe words, Emma?"

"Yellow and chief, Master Jack."

"Good girl, sweetie."

Master Jack's praise gave her the strength to endure for him. She wanted to please him and make him proud of her. Why she needed to do that she wasn't quite certain, but at that moment it became almost imperative.

As each tendril flicked against her skin, more and more endorphins released into her bloodstream until Emma felt like she was floating on a cloud. She was only aware of Master Jack as he played her body. And then more hands touched her. Master Gary moved in close to her back, his jeans slightly abrasive against her hot ass, and Master Tank moved in at her side until he, too, was touching her. Large, warm hands cupped and lifted her breasts. Fingers pinched one nipple while the other was encased in a warm, wet mouth and suckled hard. The thing hitting her moved down her front, lower and lower until it was tapping against her mound.

"Come for me, Emma," Master Jack demanded in a raspy voice.

The thing hit right between her legs, catching her engorged, achy clit. Emma was only vaguely aware of throwing her head back and bumping it against Master Gary's chest as she screamed with pleasure. Her pussy clamped and released, forcing fluid out onto her thighs. Another tap landed on her clit and Emma cried out as her body was swept away in a maelstrom of rapture. The climax was so great that her knees buckled, and she shook and shuddered with nirvana. Never in her life had she experienced such ecstasy.

The trembling finally slowed, and she became aware of firm arms holding her up so she wouldn't hurt her arms and wrists. Then someone's hands were at her wrists and ankles as she was released from the restraints.

They massaged her shoulder joints as her arms were slowly lowered down next to her sides. Something soft and warm was wrapped around her body, and then someone removed the blindfold. Emma kept her eyes closed as she basked in satiation, not wanting to face the stark light of reality just yet. She was lifted up into strong arms and carried. The gentle rocking motion was soothing, and she rested her head on Master Tank's shoulder. The movement stopped, and then she was embraced in heat and comfort as Master Tank cuddled her on his lap.

Masters Jack and Gary were sitting on either side of her, running their hands up and down her arms and legs as Master Tank soothed her. Emma felt loved and cherished, and she wanted to continue to bask in their attention. But slowly the noises of the club began to penetrate her foggy mind and she remembered why she was here.

When she opened her eyes, her men were watching her intently. She took a quick glance around and saw that they were sitting in one of the semi-secluded seating areas. Master Jack clasped her hand, raised it to his mouth, and kissed the back of it. "How are you feeling, sweetie?"

"I–I…" Emma sighed because she couldn't think enough to answer.

"That good, huh?"

"Yeah."

Master Gary handed her an open bottle of water. "Drink, Emma. You need to keep hydrated."

Emma took the bottle and drank deeply. She hadn't realized how thirsty she was until the first sip. Before she knew it, half the water was gone.

"That's my girl." Master Tank kissed the top of her head and rubbed his cheek over her hair.

"Now that you've experienced your first real foray into BDSM, what do you think, Emma?" Master Gary took the bottled water from her hand and placed it on the small table in front of the sofa.

"I want to try more." She answered without hesitation.

"We're glad you liked it, baby. Don't you worry, there is so much more we have yet to show you. Do you want to stay and watch for a while, or would you like to go home?"

"Can we stay for a bit?"

"Sure we can, darlin'. If you have any questions about what you see, just ask, okay?" Master Tank squeezed her waist.

"Okay, Master."

Emma watched as subs walked behind their Doms. One poor woman had a collar around her throat with a leash attached to it. The Dom was leading her along, but she was crawling along on her hands and knees. She felt sorry for the poor woman and hoped she never pissed her men off enough to make her do that. Emma was just about to ask why a Dom would treat her sub that way when a ruckus across the other side of the room caught her attention. Masters Gary and Jack immediately rose to their feet and headed toward the commotion.

"Will you be all right here by yourself for a moment, darlin'? It looks like they could use my help." Master Tank lifted her onto the cushion beside him.

"I'll be fine, Master."

He turned and gave her a stern look. "Don't move from that spot, little sub."

"I won't, Master Tank. I promise."

"Such a good little sub." Master Tank stroked her hair and then hurried over to the other side of the room.

Emma couldn't really see what was happening, but from the tall, angry man yelling, it didn't look good. She settled back into the corner of the sofa and looked about while she waited for her men to come back for her.

A noise behind the tall screen off to her right caused her to turn her head. A man she had never seen before leered at her. Emma recoiled. He leaned forward, reaching for her, and the light shone off his bald head. *Wait, I* have *seen him before!* She recognized him from the club on her first day here. She'd even spoken to him face-to-face at the house when he delivered some papers for Gary. Before she could figure out why he was here, he grabbed her hair, pulling her head back to an awkward angle. Emma drew breath to yell for help but a white cloth covered her mouth and nose. She gasped in fear. A sickly sweet smell assailed her nostrils, and she began to feel light-headed. Her vision blurred, and she felt her body slumping toward the ground. The cloth was removed from her face, and then arms lifted her up. She was being carried toward an emergency exit door nearby.

Emma knew she was in trouble and tried to fight off the fog, but she couldn't even get her mouth to cooperate with her brain let alone control her arms or legs. The door burst open, and she shivered as a cool breeze washed over her. She tried to fight him, but she didn't stand a chance. He was too big and she was too groggy.

He carried her toward a four-wheel drive SUV that was already running with the front and passenger doors wide open. The bastard threw her into the backseat, and she cried out with fear and pain as her forehead connected with the metal doorframe. She landed on the seat and clutched her throbbing head as the door slammed closed behind her.

The other door shut with a loud bang and then the vehicle was careening into the street. When the pain in her head dulled to a loud throb, Emma removed her hands and stared at her blood-covered hands with incomprehension.

And then stark terror permeated her body when she heard a voice from the driver's seat.

"Did you think you could escape me forever, you little slut?"

Chapter Thirteen

Gary helped deal with the three wannabe Doms as they fought over a sub. The poor woman was so scared she was shaking. Jack tended to the sub, making sure she was okay and trying to get her to calm down.

When the ruckus had started he was worried that more than three men had been involved but was thankful to see that the monitors had the situation well in hand. Two monitors who were also fully trained Doms pulled them apart and Barry also stepped in. Just as Gary turned to go back to Emma, he spotted Tank heading over.

"Where's Emma?" Gary snapped.

"She's fine. She promised to stay on the sofa and not move. No one can get her unless they go past us first, and Mike was given a photo of Mitchell. There is no way in hell that asshole will get in here."

Just as Tank finished speaking, all their cell phones rang. Gary frowned, and when he looked at the display and saw the number, he spun around and hurried back to Emma as he answered his call. His knees nearly buckled when he spotted the empty sofa. He didn't even give Turner's security monitor a chance to speak.

"Where is she?"

"One of the delivery guys took her."

"Where?"

"Out the emergency exit near where you are now."

"Fuck! How the hell could this happen with so many people in here?" Gary snarled.

"I'm sorry, Gary, but everyone's attention was across the other side of the room where the guest Doms were fighting over the little sub."

"Did you see the vehicle?" Gary asked as he burst out the emergency door with Tank close on his heels.

"Yeah, I have the license plate." Tom the security guy rattled off the number and gave him a description of the SUV.

"Thank God for small mercies. I'm going to hang up now so I can call in reinforcements and put out an APB on the SUV."

"Wait," Tom said. "I was able to blow up the image of the driver. That delivery guy drove in, but once he got out, another man jumped out of the back and got behind the wheel. It's that guy you were looking for."

"Jesus! Call me if you find out anything else. Thanks, Tom." Gary disconnected the call. Jack came sprinting out the side door moments later, his medical bag in hand. Gary filled him in on the little information he had as the three of them headed for his truck. "Mitchell's not working alone anymore. He must have bought off this deliveryman."

"What about the officers you put in the lot to watch for Mitchell?" Jack asked.

"He must have hidden in the back. They didn't see him." He yanked open the driver's side door. "But they're chasing him now." Gary gunned the engine, talking on his police radio as he drove like a bat out of hell.

"Do you have any idea where this fucker will take her?" Jack asked.

"No, but we won't stop looking until we get her back."

Just as Gary finished speaking, a voice came over the radio. He reached down and turned up the volume. Mitchell's SUV had been spotted heading in a northwest direction and had just hit the NW Sunset Highway. Tank reached out and flicked the switch for the lights and siren. Gary zipped through traffic and planted his foot on the accelerator, hoping that the fucker wasn't headed toward one of the small airports on the outskirts of town.

* * * *

Emma clutched at the door handle as Andrew swerved through traffic at a high speed. If she hadn't, she would have been thrown across the other side of the car. Her head was still swimming and her vision was blurry. She didn't know if that was because of what was on the cloth earlier or from when her head had slammed into the door frame, not that it mattered at that point. Even though she was feeling sick to her stomach and the pain in her head was still bad, it had dulled a little and she was able to think. Being careful not to give herself away, she lifted her head from the seat and looked at the lock on the door. It wasn't engaged.

When the car swerved again, she pushed aside the thought of jumping from a speeding vehicle. With her luck she would land on the road in front of another car and get run over.

"The bitch is awake."

Emma looked up to see the man who had abducted her watching her over the back of the front seat. He leered at her body, and she pulled the blanket tighter, trying to hide her nakedness from view. She tucked one end in between her breasts and glared at the asshole.

She'd seen him before, but what was he doing here? Was he a friend of Andrew's?

The man answered that question for her when he turned to Andrew. "You forked over ten thousand just so I'd kidnap her? I'd have done it just for five minutes with this little beauty. I still get to take her first, right?"

"Right," Andrew grunted, his attention on driving.

Neither of you will lay a hand on me. This wasn't going to be like last time, Emma resolved. She was up against two men this time, but she was going to keep her wits about her.

Hearing sirens in the distance, she struggled to pull herself into an upright position. Her stomach roiled, protesting the movement, as did her throbbing head. Emma reached up when she felt warm moisture trickling down her nose and wiped it away. The blood on her hands was testament that her head was still bleeding, albeit a bit slower. With care she turned to look out the back of the SUV and was pleased to see two police cars giving chase. When she turned back she was thrown across the other side of the vehicle as Andrew swerved around a truck into oncoming traffic.

"Are you crazy?" Emma yelled and clung to the handle above the door. "Are you trying to get us all killed? If you pull over now and surrender, the police will go a lot easier on you."

Andrew ignored her and careened back onto the right side of the road. Emma let out a sigh, but her relief was short lived. The next thing she knew, the SUV lurched into the gravel on the side of the road and the rear end of the car swung out. It teetered on two wheels for what seemed like minutes, but Emma knew it was actually tenths of a second. Everything seemed to happen in slow motion.

The SUV tipped up onto its side, sliding on the tarmac. The sounds of metal crumpling and glass breaking were so loud they drowned out everything else. Emma screamed, but she couldn't hear her own voice as glass rained down over her. She clung to the handle above the door, her only lifeline in a world gone topsy-turvy. Her shoulder felt like it was about to pulled out of its socket as the vehicle rolled and rolled again. Her body hit the roof, and she covered her already injured head with her free arm, trying to protect her head and face as the vehicle continued to roll.

A loud bang and the crunch of more metal rang in her ears, and sparks flew by as the steel frame of the SUV scraped along the road. When the car finally slowed and came to a stop, Emma's ears were ringing and the smell of gas filled her nostrils. She groaned when she let go of the handle. Her arm was throbbing and her shoulder ached from being wrenched so hard. She blinked a few times but could only see blurry light. *Did I hit my head again?*

Then she realized her eyes were covered in a thick, sticky substance. She wiped them with her hands, which came away covered in blood. Emma tried to keep the panic at bay by inhaling deeply as she took stock of her body. She wiggled her toes then shifted her legs.

So far, so good. Her body ached from head to toe and her head was pounding like a jackhammer was lodged in her brain, but she was alive.

The scent of gas became stronger, and Emma knew she had to get out. She looked about and cringed when her neck protested, but she spied the broken window nearby and began to carefully crawl forward. She didn't have to travel far before her head poked out of the opening.

"Ma'am, are you okay?"

Emma looked up into the worried face of a police officer. He reached in and gently helped her out of the destroyed vehicle.

"Can you hear me, miss?" the officer asked as he wrapped her in a silver thermal blanket and then lifted her into his arms.

"Y–Yes," Emma answered as best she could. Now that she was away from Andrew Mitchell and out of the car, reaction set in. She was cold to her bones and shaking like a leaf. She tried to stop the tremors running through her body, but it didn't make any difference. The harder she tried to stop the quakes, the worse they got. The officer rushed her over to the side of the road and gently placed her on a patch of grass.

"Don't move, ma'am. Paramedics are on their way." He turned away. "I have to see if I can get the other two people out of the car."

Before he finished speaking, there was a loud explosion. Heat and debris flew into the air. If Emma had been standing, she would have been knocked to the ground. The officer dove for her and covered her with his larger body. Emma held in the scream as he hit her hard. Her ribs protested as did every other bone in her body. The officer lifted off of her.

"Sorry, miss. The blast threw me."

"'S okay," Emma managed to slur just before she let the world spin away and blessed darkness beckoned.

* * * *

"Can you see the SUV yet?" Gary asked as they virtually flew past cars which moved out of their way.

"No," Tank replied as he scanned.

"How far behind are we?" Jack asked from the back seat.

"No more than a minute," Gary answered.

Tank listened to the police radio and cringed when the officers chasing Mitchell said the idiot had swerved into oncoming traffic.

"Can't you go any faster?" Tank snarled at Gary. "Sorry, don't answer that. You're doing the best you can with all the other cars on the road."

Gary didn't reply and Tank knew it was taking all of his friend's concentration to weave through the stream of cars as they got out of the way.

Another report came over the radio. Tank gripped the dashboard and seat until his knuckles turned white as he listened to the police officer describe how the SUV lost control and started to roll. Pain lanced his chest and fear permeated his soul for Emma's safety.

Another officer's voice came over the police band. "We need paramedics and the fire department on site."

"Fuck!" Jack yelled from the backseat as the accident site came into view.

There was a long line of cars but most had pulled off onto the shoulder of the road.

Gary was able to get within fifty yards of where the smoke and fire lit up the night sky. He slammed on the brakes, and as soon as the truck stopped, Tank jumped from the cab and ran. He could hear Jack pounding the asphalt behind him and knew Gary would be following, too. Tank's legs buckled and he went down onto his knees when he saw that the SUV was engulfed in flame.

There was no way anyone could survive burning alive. Tank's eyes filled with tears and he was only vaguely aware of the tortured roar from the man beside him. Jack gripped his shoulder as he, too, went down to his knees. Gary had halted on his other side, his face pale. He hands clenched in fists so tight they were turning white, and Tank could hear him grinding his teeth as he tried to control his anguish. Grief pierced his heart and he was about to lose total control of his emotions, but a glint off to the side of the road caught his attention.

Tank looked over to see an officer moving off a small female body covered in a silver thermal blanket. The auburn-colored hair shone in the headlights from a car. Even though her face was covered with blood, he knew it was Emma.

"Jack, Gary, she's alive," Tank rasped out of a throat tight with emotion and gripped Jack's shoulder. "Get it together, man, our woman needs you."

Tank pointed to the gap between two cars at the side of the road. He rose to his feet and helped Jack stand, looking at Gary to make sure he had heard. The three of them sprinted over to their woman. Emma was covered in blood, and from what he could see she was as white as a ghost beneath the red, but he saw the silver blanket rise as she took a breath. Their little darlin' was alive.

Jack opened his bag and began to assess Emma. "She bruised all over and has a laceration on her forehead." Tank held his breath as Jack examined Emma's neck and then lifted her eyelids and shined a small torch into her eyes. "I think she has a concussion and possibly whiplash and her ribs are bruised, possibly fractured."

Tank watched as Jack took her blood pressure.

"Her blood pressure is low, which could be caused by internal bleeding or shock. I'm going to set up an IV and give her something for pain." He stood up and shouted for the paramedics, who had pulled up not far behind them.

Tank had never been so glad that Jack was a surgeon. He worked tirelessly, checking Emma over thoroughly and directing the paramedics. He and Gary kept out of the way.

Within minutes Jack and the paramedics had a brace around her neck and a backboard beneath her to support her spine, and then they carefully loaded her onto the portable gurney.

"I'll call as soon as I know how she's doing," Jack yelled as he followed the paramedics to the ambulance. Tank wanted to get in the truck and follow, but first he and Gary had to deal with the officers.

It was going to be a long night, but he didn't care. As long as Emma was alive, that was all that mattered.

Chapter Fourteen

Emma frowned because the beeping wouldn't stop. The noise was driving her crazy and causing her head to ache even more. She shifted her arm and felt a slight sting in her hand, as if something was piercing her skin. She wanted to open her eyes, but her eyelids were heavy and wouldn't obey her command. A moan sounded close by and she realized she had made the sound. Her whole body ached and throbbed, and she wondered what had happened. She tried to remember, but concentrating just made the pounding in her head intensify. Darkness consumed her again, and she relaxed and let it pull her back into the bliss where there was no pain.

When she surfaced again, she was more aware of her surroundings. She had no idea how much time had passed since she last became semiconscious. Large, warm hands gripped both of hers and she wanted to see who was beside her. The hum of a machine drew her attention, and she whimpered when a tight band began to crush her arm.

"Shh, Emma, you're safe, baby. You're in the hospital." A hand stroked her hair and she sighed with contentment. She knew that voice and touch.

"Gary?" she croaked.

"Yeah, baby, I'm here."

"We won't leave your side, darlin'," a deep, gravelly voice chimed in from her other side.

"Tank?" Emma licked her dry lips.

"Yes, Emma. Just rest, darlin'. The more you rest, the faster you'll heal."

"Thirsty."

Something touched her lips and Emma opened her mouth. A straw was pushed into her mouth and she sucked the liquid up until her mouth was once more moist. There was a slight swishing sound and the air moved. Emma tried to pry her eyelids open but the feat was beyond her.

"Emma, how are you feeling, sweetie?"

"Jack?"

"Yes, sweetie, it's me. Can you open your eyes for me, Emma?"

Emma concentrated on opening her eyes, and her eyelids finally lifted so she could see through mere slits. The light was too bright and hurt her head. She sobbed with pain and closed her eyes again.

"Good girl, Emma. You're going to be fine, sweetie. Just rest and let your body heal."

Each day she felt better. Knowing that Andrew Mitchell would never be able to come after her again helped her relax. She wouldn't have wished him dead, but knowing that she was safe lifted a weight from her shoulders. Gary had informed her that the vehicle had exploded before the police officers could get him and his friend out of the wreck. They had died at the scene.

Emma spent a total of a week in the hospital. She had been lucky and had suffered no broken bones. Other than being stiff and sore and suffering from headaches and whiplash, she had suffered no adverse effects. At least one of her men was with her all the time. Jack stopped in to check up on her regularly, at least five times a day, since she was in the hospital he worked at.

By the end of the week Emma was chomping at the bit to leave. She found it hard to sleep in the hospital now that she was almost well. The noise was constant. She didn't complain, but she really just wanted to go home and sleep in her own bed again.

My bed or theirs? The thought stopped her in her tracks. When her Doms visited, they didn't say anything about the future. What would she do if they took her back to her apartment?

They said they wanted me to move in with them. They even moved the furniture. But will that change now that Andrew's dead? They no longer had to protect her.

She knew she wouldn't be able to settle properly until she was back with her men, cuddled up between them, surrounded in their heat and love. If that love was gone, she might never sleep again.

Trying to set aside her worries, Emma pushed the button on the remote and sighed with relief when the top half of the bed began to tilt up. Her ass and back were going numb from being in bed so long, and she wanted to get up to shower. Although she'd had daily sponge baths given by the caring and dedicated nurses, she still felt grungy and wanted to wash her hair. Now that the needle for the IV had been taken out of her hand, she was determined to do just that.

One of the nurses had said she would help her in the bathroom in a little while, but the poor woman had rushed away when some sort of alarm had sounded. She was quite capable of washing herself, so she thought to save the nurse some time.

With care, Emma eased her legs over the side of the bed and sat up straight. She was still a little dizzy if she moved too fast, so she took things slow. Reaching up behind her, she released the clasps on the collar she was wearing and sighed with liberation. Her neck was still stiff and sore, but to have the collar off was such a respite. Emma wasn't worried about getting her stitches wet anymore because the nurse had said they would be taken out later in the day.

She moved slowly in case she got dizzy and needed to hold on to something, but she was fine. With a smile she grabbed the clothes Tank had brought from the small cupboard and made her way into the en suite bathroom.

The shower did wonders. Afterward, she peered at herself in the mirror as she brushed her hair. She felt almost back to her normal self. The stitches which marred her pale forehead didn't bother her, nor did the fact that she would have a scar above her right eyebrow. Emma was just happy to be alive.

A loud bang sounded from the room, and Emma cautiously opened the bathroom door to a crack and peered out. Jack was standing at the end of her bed and he looked really worried. She pushed the door open further and stepped into the room.

"I'm here."

"Oh, thank God." Jack rushed over and pulled her into his arms.

Emma inhaled his wonderful scent and hugged him tight around the waist. Jack lightly gripped her arms and pulled back so he could look down into her eyes.

"You are in big trouble, sweetie. You were supposed wait for help while you took a shower. What if you had become dizzy and fallen, Emma? Just wait until you are all healed. I'm going to paddle your ass good."

"What's she done now?" Gary asked as he walked into the room.

Jack explained, and Gary gave her a hard stare.

"That's one, baby. Don't think that we'll forget. When you are totally healed, we are going to punish you good."

Emma's breasts swelled and her nipples peaked. She shifted on her feet and squeezed her legs together. She couldn't wait for them to discipline her because she knew that they would all find immense pleasure as she submitted to her three sexy, dominant men.

Tank came strolling into the room with papers in his hand. He looked from Emma to Gary and Jack and back to Emma again. "What's going on?"

Emma crossed her arms and waited impatiently as Gary and Jack explained her transgression. Tank walked over to her and scooped her up into his arms. "You are in big trouble, darlin'. I can't wait until you're all better."

She wrapped her arms around his neck and kissed him long and hard, putting all her love and desire into the kiss. When she pulled back, she was pleased to see that Tank was breathing just as hard as she was and his eyes had turned dark with desire.

"Give her to me." Gary came over and took her from Tank. "Don't think that you can control us, baby. We are the Doms and you are the sub." He leaned down and then slanted his mouth over hers, kissing her hungrily.

"All right, that's enough. I need to take her stitches out and then we can go home. Put her on the bed," Jack ordered.

Gary half obeyed Jack's directive. He sat on the bed and held her on his lap with his arms around hers and her chest. He was probably worried that she would move and hurt herself while Jack removed the sutures. Emma sighed with contentment. The three men took such good care of her. She felt so loved and cherished and vowed to be the best sub she could be. Of course that meant she was going to act up because she knew they loved her just as she was and loved to mete out punishment to her. Why wouldn't they since they were all satisfied in the end?

"Okay, I'm done. Let's go home," Jack stated.

"Don't I have to sign out or something?" Emma asked.

Tank held up the papers in his hand. "All taken care of, darlin'."

Gary stood with her in his arms and headed for the door.

"Hey, I can walk." Emma palmed his cheek.

Gary nuzzled his face into her hand and then looked over at Jack.

"You have two choices. You can be carried out or go out in a wheelchair." He indicated the chair waiting just outside the door.

Emma decided not to argue because she could see by the determined look in her men's eyes that she wasn't going to win. "I'll stay right where I am."

Gary kissed her temple and started walking again. "Good choice, baby."

* * * *

Emma was so horny her panties were in a constant state of dampness. Being near her men and not having them touch her was making her insane. She leaned against the kitchen counter with a sigh while Tank got them some water.

They still made sure she was never alone. They slept in her bed every night, and she loved going to sleep and waking up surrounded by them. But she was becoming frustrated. Emma wanted to make love with her Doms, but they had ignored all her flirting and goading. She touched them every chance she got by brushing her breasts against their arms, kissing them a lot, and when she could, hugging them tight and rubbing her body over theirs. But they were stubborn and held fast. Even when she'd been cuddling with Tank tonight and she had been rubbing her hands over his chest and belly, he'd been restrained, even though she knew he was turned on. She was ready to pull her hair out and scream the house down.

Most of the bruising from the accident had faded, and even though her neck was sometimes still stiff and she got the occasional headache, she was totally healed. Even Jack said so.

Her stomach flipped over. *If they're going to tell me to go back home, they'll do it soon.* All week she'd waited for one of the men to bring up the subject of their future, but none of them seemed to be thinking about it. And though Gary had ordered her furniture to be sent to the house, it had never showed up. Emma was too afraid to ask if that had just been a joke or if the men had changed their minds. If they had, if they were going to send her away now that she no longer needed their care and protection, she wasn't sure she wanted to know before it happened.

She wanted to make love with them. She wanted to be with them forever. And they wouldn't give her anything she wanted!

"What are you thinking about so hard?" Tank asked, squeezing her in closer to his side.

"Nothing," she answered petulantly.

Tank moved back slightly and tipped her chin up so he could see her eyes. "Did you just lie to me?"

Emma inhaled deeply and stared into his beautiful green eyes. He was looking at her with such heat, her pussy clenched and her clit throbbed. She felt as if she was drowning and he could see into her soul.

"What's going on?" Gary asked as he joined them, Jack close on his heels.

"I asked Emma a question, and she lied to me."

"Did she now?" Gary stood so close to her she could feel his body heat.

She jumped when large, warm hands landed on her shoulders.

"Sorry, sweetie, I didn't mean to startle you. I thought you knew I was behind you," Jack said.

"Emma's been getting away with too much lately. I think it's time we took our recalcitrant sub in hand," Gary said in a firm, cool voice.

Oh God. Yes, please.

Gary stepped back and gave her gave her a hard stare, but she could see the heat in his eyes as he lowered his gaze and perused her body.

"Stand up, sub," Master Gary ordered.

Emma's insides heated and cream leaked from her pussy. She straightened and lowered her head.

"Strip, Emma," Master Tank commanded.

Emma's stomach fluttered with excitement. Her body was screaming that they hurry up and touch her, but she knew that if she begged or demanded they would draw things out. She was so needy she was shaking with desire. Taking care not to look too desperate, Emma pulled her T-shirt over her head and dropped it on the floor. She then unhooked her bra and it, too, got discarded. With shaking hands she pushed her sweatpants over her hips, down her legs, and off. She had never been happier than she was right now that she hadn't bothered to put any panties on that morning.

"Assume the position, little sub," Master Jack demanded in a husky voice.

Emma was glad that her men weren't as immune to her as they pretended. Master Jack's breathlessness had given him away. She kneeled down and sat on her heels, keeping her eyes lowered, and then placed her hands on her thighs, palms up.

"You are in so much trouble, sugar." Master Gary approached until the tips of his shoes came within sight. "Do you think we don't know you've been trying to get us to make love with you?"

"You've been racking up the punishments, sweetie." Master Jack came around the sofa until his shoes were also in sight.

She heard movement beside her as Master Tank rose. "How many is she up to now?" he asked.

"At least twenty swats," Master Jack answered.

"Twenty. I thought the last count was ten?" Master Tank asked.

"Yeah, it was, but I remembered how she showered in the hospital by herself. She was supposed to wait for the nurse."

"Twenty it is," Master Gary affirmed. "Stand up, Emma."

Emma got to her feet and waited for her next command. She shivered as the cool air caressed her naked body, and she pressed her legs together to relieve her aching pussy. Her thighs were wet with her juices.

Smack.

Ow! That hurt. Emma didn't say anything though because she knew it would earn her another tap on the ass.

"Stop squeezing your legs together, little sub," Master Tank said in a growly voice. "We will decide when you receive your pleasure."

"Follow me, sub." Master Gary turned and headed down the hallway.

Emma followed him but kept her eyes down. She was already looking at twenty smacks and didn't want to add to her punishment. A gasp of excitement bubbled up in her chest when Master Gary led her to the play room, but she was able to contain the sound. She followed him into the dungeon and stood with her hands behind her back, knowing how her Doms loved to see her breasts pushed out. Masters

Tank and Jack entered the room. She heard one of them close the door, and the lock engaged with a loud *snick.*

"Very pretty, Emma." Master Gary turned to face her. She could see him from beneath her lowered eyelashes.

"Get on the spanking bench, sweetie," Master Jack ordered and gave her a little shove toward the piece of furniture.

Emma got onto the bench and wiggled until she was comfortable. Another slap landed on her ass.

"Don't move, sub," Master Tank growled.

Warm, large hands secured her to the bench. The cuffs around her wrists and thighs were lined with fur so they wouldn't abrade her skin. Another wide, fur-lined strap was placed over her back and secured to the bench. She was totally at their mercy, just where she loved to be.

Three sets of hands stroked and caressed over her whole body. Emma's breathing escalated, as did her heartbeat. She couldn't wait until her punishment was over because she knew that once it was, her men would make love with her. Cream dripped onto her thighs, and she tried to relax and control her desire, but she had waited so long and was so needy for her men, it wouldn't slow.

"We are going to give you ten slaps by hand, Emma, and then Master Tank will give you ten using the flogger," Master Gary informed her.

Yes. Please hurry. Emma loved it when the tendrils of the flogger landed on her skin. She had come so hard when Master Jack had used it on her at the club.

Smack. Smack. Smack. Smack. Smack.

Emma moaned as the sting from the slaps warmed her ass and made her clit tingle. Her pussy clenched as if begging to be filled. A large hand rubbed over her heated skin.

"Good girl," Master Gary praised. "You like it when we spank you, don't you, Emma?"

"Yes, Master Gary."

"Such a good little sub."

Smack. Smack. Smack. Smack. Smack.

Emma sobbed as the stinging pain morphed into pleasure. The last five swats were from Master Jack's hand. His slaps always seemed to sting more than Master Gary's, since he seemed to flick his wrist rather than paddle her with his whole hand like Master Gary did.

"Very good, sweetie. You've made me happy by taking your punishment."

She felt a breeze on her ass and Master Tank's unique manly scent drifted to her nostrils. She inhaled deeply and waited for his punishment. He ran his hands over her hot ass as Master Gary and Master Jack stroked up and down her arms, legs, and back. Her clit throbbed and her nipples ached.

"You are not to come, Emma. If you do I will shove a vibrator in your pussy and bring you to the brink of orgasm over and over again without letting you climax until you beg me to fuck you. Do you understand, darlin'?"

"Yes, Master Tank."

"Such a pretty little sub."

Emma waited for Master Tank to begin whipping her with the flogger. The longer she waited, the more her muscles tensed with anticipation. She jumped when the first flick landed and the tendrils of suede connected with her flesh. Each time it connected with her skin, Emma relaxed more and more until she was floating on a cloud. The love of her men surrounded her, and she was free to give up control.

The thuds to her skin stopped, and she sighed with contentment. She had pleased Master Tank by not climaxing. Someone removed the restraints and then she was lifted from the bench.

"I think it's time our good little sub was rewarded." Master Tank's voice came from above her head.

Emma wrapped her arms around his neck and held on tight. He carried her across the room, and then Masters Jack and Gary helped him lift and position her. Her eyes snapped open, and she moaned as she was lowered onto the funny-looking seat protruding from the wall. The dildo sticking up from the middle stretched and filled her sheath as her Doms lowered her. Masters Tank and Gary spread her arms out wide above her head and shackled her wrists. Master Jack did the same with her legs and secured her ankles. Her whole weight was on the dildo and seat, and she couldn't move.

They moved away and stood in front of her. Master Gary held up what looked like a remote control and then pressed one of the buttons with his thumb. Emma whimpered as the dildo began to vibrate. She wanted to raise and lower herself on it, but she was held firm. She twitched her hips and tried to get the vibrator to massage her G-spot, but she couldn't move enough.

She looked up at Master Gary when he chuckled, and then his thumb moved again as he pushed another button. Emma gasped as another part of the seat began to vibrate. This one was directly on her clit. Her pussy rippled and spasmed, and she panted, trying to stave off the impending climax.

"Come, Emma," Master Tank demanded.

Emma screamed as her internal muscles continuously contracted. Just when she thought her climax had finished, the vibrations got stronger and sent her over into another orgasm. Her whole body shook and shuddered, her pussy clenched and released until cum gushed from her cunt. The vibrations stopped and then hands quickly released the cuffs.

"You are so fucking sexy, Emma," Master Tank said as he carefully lifted her from the dildo and carried her across the room. "I love you, darlin'."

Emma rested her head on his shoulder with a satisfied smile. "I love you, too."

She wiggled closer to him, feeling how hard he was. "Will you all make love to me now?"

"Not yet."

Emma lifted her head. Her happiness dissolved. She blurted, "You're going to send me away, aren't you?"

She couldn't have said which of the men looked more surprised. "Send you where, sweetie?" Jack asked.

At almost the same time, Gary said, "But you live with us."

"You said I would move in with you, but where's my furniture?" she asked.

"It's in storage," Tank said. "We were waiting until your injuries were better before we bothered you about all that stuff. Baby, you didn't think we'd changed our minds, did you?"

Since that was exactly what she'd thought, Emma kept her mouth shut. Her heart was beating hard with a combination of relief and leftover fear.

Gary turned her face toward his with his fingertips. "I think our little sub will need to be punished for doubting us. But not tonight."

He put her on her feet, and Jack handed her the clothes she'd dropped in the other room. "Right now we have other plans for you," he said. "Get dressed."

Chapter Fifteen

Emma stood on the stage in the middle of the great room of the Club of Dominance with her head and eyes lowered. The stage was surrounded by people waiting to see what her men were going to do. She wished she knew but she didn't have a clue. After she had cleaned up and dressed, they had all bundled into Master Tank's car and now here she was.

She was fully dressed in a black leather miniskirt and red corset. She leaned back into Master Jack as he hugged her from behind. Nervous excitement caused her to shiver, and Master Jack gave her a reassuring squeeze. Masters Gary and Tank were standing on either side of her.

"I want to thank you all for coming. We want you to meet our sub, Emma. She is one special sexy lady."

Love filled Emma's heart, and her cheeks grew warm at Master Gary's praise. Master Jack released her and walked around to stand in front of her. Masters Gary and Tank moved until they, too, were standing with their backs to the crowd and facing her.

Master Tank moved first and got down on his knees. Masters Jack and Gary followed, and each of them took one of her hands in theirs. Master Tank cleared his throat nervously and looked into her eyes.

"Emma, I have never been happier in my life. You mean the world to me, darlin'. I love you so much."

Moisture filled Emma's eyes and spilled over her lower lids. She pulled her hand from Master Gary's, reached out, and cupped Master Tank's cheek. "I love you, too."

Master Jack lifted her hand to his mouth and kissed the back of it. "I love you, sweetie. You are every breath I take."

"I love you, Jack...Master Jack," Emma quickly amended and laughter rippled through the room.

Master Gary drew her attention by clasping her hand again, and he squeezed it. "Emma, I am so happy you came into my life. My life would have no meaning if you weren't here with me. I love you, little sub."

Tears streamed down Emma's cheeks, and she sobbed with joy. "I love you so much."

Master Tank lifted his arm and held out a gold choker which had three diamonds embedded into it. "Will you do us the honor of being our permanent sub, darlin'?"

Emma knelt down and stared through blurry, moisture-filled eyes. "I would be proud to be a sub to you all."

Cheers and whistles rang through the room as Master Tank fitted the choker around her neck. Emma moved in closer to her men and sighed as they all hugged her together. The noise finally died down and her Doms helped her to stand.

Master Gary held her hand and began to speak again. "Emma, we've already discussed it between the three of us and are happy with the outcome."

Emma had no idea what he was talking about and wanted to ask but waited patiently instead.

Again her three men got down on their knees. "Emma, would you marry us? You would marry me on paper since I'm the eldest, but you would be the wife of all us if you accept."

Emma squealed and launched herself at her men. "Yes. Yes. Yes, I will marry you all."

The crowd roared and clapped again. Master Gary scooped her up into his arms and headed toward the back of the room, where Master Turner was smiling and holding the door to his private rooms open.

"Congratulations, Emma." Master Turner smiled at her and then looked at Master Gary. "You may stay as long as you wish."

Emma snuggled into Master Gary's neck and sighed with happiness. He carried her into the room where she had first met her three Doms. Master Gary lowered her to her feet and stepped back.

"Strip."

Emma practically ripped her clothes off in her hurry to get naked. When she looked up she saw her men were also disrobing.

Master Tank pulled her back against his naked front. He kissed her neck, cupped her breasts, and then plucked at her nipples. "Tonight we are your fiancés and not your Doms. We want to make love with you and make you feel good, darlin'."

"Yes," Emma sighed.

Jack came up to her and palmed her cheeks in her hands. He leaned down and kissed her hungrily. Emma wrapped her hand around his hard cock. He groaned into her mouth and thrust his hips forward.

"Get her on the bed," Gary rasped.

Jack picked her up and carried her to the bed. He lay down in the middle of the mattress on his back, taking her with him, and then slanted his mouth over hers again and again. Emma mewled when Tank and Gary got on the bed and caressed her flesh. She thrust her breasts forward and moaned when her nipples were pinched. One of the men gripped her hips and raised her up onto her knees so she was straddling Jack's pelvis. Fingers dipped into her pussy and stroked the length of her slit until finally settling on her clit. Emma groaned. Her pussy clenched, and cream leaked from her vagina.

"Take Jack inside you, darlin'," Tank ordered in a breathless voice.

Emma shifted until she the tip of Jack's cock touched her hole and then she lowered down as he pushed up. They both moaned as his hard dick filled her pussy.

"You feel like heaven, sweetie. Your pussy is so hot, wet, and tight." Jack pulled her down onto his chest when he was buried in her body balls-deep.

Cold liquid dribbled down her ass crack and onto her anus. Emma clenched reflexively, which earned a gentle swat to the ass. "Don't clench, darlin'. Try and stay relaxed for me." Tank eased a finger into her anus and coated her rectum with lube. He took his time and stretched her out until she was moaning and taking three fingers.

"Use your muscles and push out for me, Emma." Tank gently thrust the head of his cock into her rosette until the corona popped through her ring of muscles. "So fucking good. Her ass is gripping my cock so hard."

Emma shivered and mewled with pleasure as Tank slowly worked his cock into her dark entrance. By the time he was embedded inside her she was on the verge of coming. She was stuffed so full of cock, but she needed more. With Jack and Tank's help she sat up and looked to her side. Gary was ready and waiting for her, on his knees with his hand wrapped around his hard shaft. Emma leaned over and licked his mushroom-shaped head. He groaned when she dipped her tongue into the slit and tasted his yummy pre-cum. She slid her mouth down over his erection, and as she pulled back up, she hollowed her cheeks.

Jack and Tank started to move with slow pumps of their hips. As Tank withdrew from her ass, Jack surged forward into her pussy. Emma got into a rhythm, bobbing up and down Gary's penis, and as she retreated, she made sure to lave the sensitive underside of his dick with her tongue. Emma reached out and gripped Gary's cock. The diamond ring of her finger sparkled in the overhead light and love filled her heart. These men were no longer just Doms playing with a sub. They were *her* Doms and she was *their* sub. But most importantly they were *her husbands-to-be*.

With each stroke of their cocks, Emma's internal muscles rippled and tautened. The friction they created as they caressed her inside had her on the brink of orgasm. Gary gripped her hair and tugged on it slightly, adding to her bliss as she pleasured him with her mouth.

"Fuck, Emma. You've got me there. I'm gonna come, baby. Swallow me down."

Emma took Gary's cock to the back of her throat and swallowed. Gary roared. His cock expanded and pulsed, and his cum shot from the end of his dick, filling her mouth and throat. She drank him down with relish. When his penis began to soften, he withdrew from her mouth and bent over with his hands on his knees as he gasped for breath.

Her pussy coiled in tighter, and she covered Jack's cock with her cream.

"I can't last much longer," Tank gasped. "Send her over."

Jack reached down between their bodies and tapped her clit. That was all it took. Emma threw back her head and screamed as wave upon wave of rapture swept over her. Her pussy gripped and released, clenched and let go, over and over.

Jack and Tank shoved into her at the same time. Tank shouted as he, too, reached climax. His cock jerked in her ass as he filled her with his cum. Two thrusts later, Jack gripped her hips and yelled his release. His dick pulsed, and ropes of semen spewed from the end of his penis.

Emma flopped down onto Jack, the occasional shudder and tremor causing her pussy to twitch. Tank leaned over her from behind and Gary clasped her hand in his.

Emma was wrapped in the love of her three Dominant saviors and knew she wouldn't want to be anywhere else. There was so much to look forward to.

She couldn't wait to start the rest of her life with the men she loved.

THE END

WWW.BECCAVAN-EROTICROMANCE.COM

ABOUT THE AUTHOR

My name is Becca Van. I live in Australia with my wonderful hubby of many years, as well as my two children.

I read my first romance, which I found in the school library, at the age of thirteen and haven't stopped reading them since. It is so wonderful to know that love is still alive and strong when there seems to be so much conflict in the world.

I dreamed of writing my own book one day but, unfortunately, didn't follow my dream for many years. But once I started I knew writing was what I wanted to continue doing.

I love to escape from the world and curl up with a good romance, to see how the characters unfold and conflict is dealt with. I have read many books and love all facets of the romance genre, from historical to erotic romance. I am a sucker for a happy ending.

For all titles by Becca Van, please visit
www.bookstrand.com/becca-van

Siren Publishing, Inc.
www.SirenPublishing.com

Lightning Source UK Ltd.
Milton Keynes UK
UKOW03f1853160913

217317UK00020B/1286/P